PURRFECT PERIL

THE MYSTERIES OF MAX 7

NIC SAINT

PURRFECT PERIL

The Mysteries of Max 7

Copyright © 2018 by Nic Saint

Edited by Chereese Graves

www.nicsaint.com

Give feedback on the book at: info@nicsaint.com

facebook.com/nicsaintauthor
@nicsaintauthor

First Edition

Printed in the U.S.A

PROLOGUE

urt Goldsmith poured another bottle of bubbly over his head, the effervescent gold nectar fizzing as it hit his mane, trickled down his trim physique, and splashed across the floor of the shower cabin. He rubbed the expensive liquor into his remarkably well-preserved face—remarkable for a seventy-eight-year-old—and his thick thatch of white hair—another astonishing feat—and sighed contentedly. Other, lesser people might enjoy rubbing conditioner into their scalp but as the reigning Most Fascinating Man in the World he preferred a substance somewhat less mundane. A nice bottle of Moët & Chandon served his purposes just fine. He would have preferred Piper-Heidsieck but the hotel he was currently gracing with his exclusive presence had run out of his favorite brand so the Moët would have to do.

And it did. As soon as he'd splashed the contents of a second bottle across the remainder of his corpus, he was ready to face another day. He stepped from the pink marble shower into the pink marble bathroom and strode confidently into the adjoining bedroom, not bothering with a towel, sprightly moving to the window overlooking Hampton Cove's busiest street. He didn't go so far as to step out onto the balcony to greet the milling throngs below, but he did fling the window wide and sampled a lungful of air, planting his feet wide, hands on his thighs. The Most Fascinating Man in the World didn't do towels. The Most Fascinating Man in the World air-dried.

As he stood there, his white hair flapping in the breeze like a lion's mane, he glanced to the side table that book-ended the bed and noticed a silver salver with a single bottle of beer and a note. He remembered hearing the room service person announcing his arrival and shouting him in from the bathroom. He hadn't ordered room service, but figured another fan had left him another little present. His lady fans were always sending him personal items like edible panties or lacy little things accompanied by cheeky invitations to join them for lunch or dinner or—even more interestingly—into their boudoir.

The bottle of beer disappointed him. At first he presumed Tracy Sting had sent it up. A reminder of their lunch date. Tracy represented Dos Siglas, the well-known Mexican beer brand for whom Burt had made the popular Most Fascinating Man in the World commercials for the past fifteen years. He'd come to the Hamptons to shoot another commercial and Tracy was here to set everything up and make sure Burt had everything he needed and more. His idea of more, however, wasn't a bottle of Dos Siglas. Personally he despised the stuff. Dishwater, he liked to call it. After all, beer was the drink of the plebs. He preferred champagne, the nectar of the gods and godly men like Burt Goldsmith.

As he stood there, his hairy chest thrust out, he suddenly noticed there was something off about this particular bottle. It didn't have the typical slender shape of Dos Siglas. Instead it was squat and plump, like a bottle of Tres Siglas, Dos Siglas's main competitor.

A sudden rage ripped through him. He knew who had sent him this bottle. Curt Pigott, the Most Compelling Man in the World. A man openly challenging his dominion as the world's premier interesting man at every turn. A man dying to steal his crown. He growled a few words unfit for print under his breath, his very short and very manly beard bristling with rage, his bronze physique shedding those final few drops of Moët & Chandon Brut Impérial, and balled his fists.

This was the third time this week Curt had done this. Taunting him. Challenging him. Trying to get under his skin.

It wouldn't work. Nothing got under the skin of the Most Fascinating Man in the World unless he sent it a personal monogrammed invitation to do so.

He crossed the floor to the side table in three powerful strides. He picked up the note, ascertaining that, yes, the bottle had indeed been sent by the Most Compelling Man in the World, and yes, it was a bottle of Tres Siglas prime ale. His dark eyes shooting sheets of flame, he crumpled up the note, picked up the bottle, which was cold to the touch, drops of condensation dappling the amber surface, and aimed it at the trashcan where it landed with a dull thud.

The explosion that blasted through the room took only milliseconds to turn the Most Fascinating Man in the World into the Most Fascinating Dead Man in the World, and Burt's nice hotel room into a conflagration of fire and fury.

CHAPTER 1

$\mathcal{O}$delia Poole walked briskly along the street, her purse hiked high, her light blond hair bouncing jauntily around her shoulders, her slender frame clad in her usual work costume of white T, jeans and sneakers. She was on her way to one of the more exciting interviews of her career as a reporter for the Hampton Cove Gazette. Perhaps even the Most Exciting Interview in the World, she thought with a slight grin, as the interviewee she was about to meet was an actor who had made a name for himself as the Most Fascinating Man in the World, featuring in dozens of well-received ad campaigns for Dos Siglas beer.

Initially her editor Dan Goory had wanted to conduct the interview, big fan as he was of Burt Goldsmith and the man's body of work. But Odelia had insisted. She couldn't wait to meet the man—the legend—the icon. She had her list of questions written out, the recording app on her phone ready, and only a few more minutes separated her from the sit-down.

She glanced up at the Hampton Cove Star, the boutique hotel in downtown Hampton Cove, located right across the street from the Vickery General Store on Main Street, where all Hampton Covians like to stock up on supplies and shoot the breeze with Wilber Vickery, store owner and one of the town's mainstays and longtime citizens.

She waved a jolly hello to Wilber, who stood greeting the customers in front of his store, and was just about to enter the hotel when a familiar figure rounded the corner and gave her a happy smile. It was the bespectacled figure of Philippe Goldsmith, Burt's grandson and the person who'd set up the interview.

She halted in her tracks and returned the young man's smile. Philippe didn't look anything like his famous grandfather. He was in his mid-twenties, pale to the point of pasty, pudgy to the point of chubby, and nerdy to the point of *Big Bang's* Sheldon Cooper awkward. Philippe dragged a hand through his straggly dark hair, pushed his horn-rimmed spectacles up his bulbous nose, and gave her a hesitant smile. "Oh, hi, Miss Poole," he said.

"Hey, Philippe. Out shopping?"

He glanced down at the bulky bag he was carrying. "Oh, right. Yes. Yeah, just picking up some supplies for my grand-dad. The man enjoys his creature comforts." He pulled a carton box from the bag. Judging from the label it held a bottle of Piper-Heidsieck champagne. He held it up. "He uses this as conditioner if you can believe it."

She arched an eyebrow. "Conditioner?"

"Yeah, he says nothing tones and moisturizes the scalp like high-quality bubbly. In fact he credits champagne as the secret ingredient that has allowed him to keep his hair so luxuriant and shiny in spite of his advanced age." He clasped a hand in front of his mouth. "Oops. I probably shouldn't have said that. Especially to a reporter such as yourself."

She laughed. "The advanced age bit or the champagne secret?"

"Both," he said with an engaging grin. "Off the record?"

She nodded, tucking away these little tidbits for later use in her article.

"For a man who's about to enter his eighth decade he looks remarkably well."

"That's definitely true," she agreed. Though she'd wondered if it was Photoshop or Hollywood trickery that made Burt Goldsmith look so ageless. Apparently it wasn't.

"Anyway, we better go up," Philippe said. "Granddad doesn't like to be kept waiting."

"I'm ready if you are."

And Philippe had just opened his mouth to retort when there was an ear-splitting bang and something seemed to explode overhead. Odelia glanced up just in time to see flames shooting out from a second-floor window and a round object being catapulted down to the sidewalk. The round object came to a full stop against her foot, and as she looked down she saw that it was nothing other than the head of Burt Goldsmith himself.

The head was smoking, as if it had been on fire, and was still wearing that typical Most Fascinating Man in the World smirk, that roguish Sean Connery glint in those dark eyes, and a bemused expression on that handsomely bearded face. Burt Goldsmith's lips were parted, as if on the verge of delivering his famous line, 'Stay cool my friends.'

And as she stared down at the grotesque head in horror, she had to agree that Philippe was right: the man was remarkably well-preserved. Only now he was also very dead.

Next to her sounded a soft yelp, and the next moment Philippe had collapsed and was lying prostrate on the sidewalk, right next to the mortal remains of his famous granddad.

The Most Fascinating Grandson in the World had fainted.

7

CHAPTER 2

I awoke with a start, a powerful sense that something was awry hanging over me like a pall. I opened one eye then the other, and yawned cavernously. I stretched my limbs and glanced up at the bed. As a rule, I like to sleep at the foot of Odelia's bed, but ever since she bought herself one of those box spring contraptions I'm having a hard time navigating my approach shot. The thing is, you hit a box spring, and the box spring hits you right back. More than once I've landed on my tush on the floor, wondering what the hell happened.

How humans manage to land on the bed and stay there is a mystery to me.

I blinked against the invading light that peeped through the curtains and wondered once more what had awakened me. As far as I knew Odelia was still sound asleep, as she should be. I'm her official wake-up call, after all, and since I'd just woken up myself, it stood to reason my human was still in bed.

So why this sense that something was wrong? And then it

hit me. The music. Odelia likes to wake up to the tunes of light pop music. Rihanna or Dua Lipa or Ariana Grande. At the moment some cowboy was crooning about being kicked in the gut by the woman he loved and lost. That didn't sound like Odelia. That sounded more like…

An awful sense of foreboding jarred my teeth like a kick to the butt.

Oh, no.

Not again.

I took the leap and landed on the bed. And what I saw there turned my blood to ice.

Chase.

Chase Kingsley.

The burly cop was lying in Odelia's bed. His long, curly brown hair draped across Odelia's pillow. His muscular body covered by Odelia's comforter. His handsome face buried in Odelia's Betty Boop pajama top.

I stared at the cop.

Suddenly, he opened one eye and stared back at me!

Man stared at cat.

Cat stared at man.

It was a moment fraught with extreme emotion, not to mention tension.

Then he yawned and stretched and slapped the empty space next to him.

He frowned in confusion. "You have any idea where…" He glanced at me and smiled a wry smile. "Why am I talking to a damn cat? Of course you don't know where Odelia is. And even if you did, you wouldn't be able to tell me, would you, little buddy?"

He patted me roughly on the head—more a prod than a pat—and swung his feet to the floor. As usual, he was dressed in nothing but a tank top and a pair of boxers, his brawny arms all biceps and triceps and who-knows-what-else-ceps. Chase Kingsley's body is all muscular bumps in all kinds of places and the kind of washboard stomach human females go all goo-goo-ga-ga over, drooling at the mouth, their spine and knees turning to jelly.

You see, Chase is my human's boyfriend, and apparently boyfriends are supposed to sleep in the beds of their girl-friends. No idea why, though according to Harriet, the cat who lives next door with Odelia's mom and dad, it might have something to do with babies.

No idea what, exactly, but I have a sneaking suspicion I'm going to find out in the near future if this keeps up. Chase has been 'sleeping over' four nights in a row now, and judging from Odelia's furtive glances in my direction, the cop just might become a fixture.

I don't mind admitting I don't like it. I liked things the way they were: just me, Odelia, and my best buddy Dooley, who also lives next door. The three of us, happy as clams.

And now this, this, this... intruder!

Blake Shelton was still wailing away in the background—he's Chase's favorite warbler. The former Sexiest Man Alive is the Hunkiest Man Alive's favorite singer. Of course he is.

Chase threw the curtains wide and sunlight streamed into the room. Then he disappeared into the bathroom and moments later the shower turned on and steam started pouring into the bedroom.

I heaved a ragged sigh and directed a nasty look at Chase's phone, where Mr. Shelton was now gibbering on and on about a hillbilly bone, whatever that was. From pure frustration my skin broke out in hives and I raised my hind paw to scratch that itch.

Suddenly, and without warning, another itch broke out, this time behind my left ear, and I raised my hind paw a little higher to address that itch, too. It was no use, though, as seemingly all across my voluminous body my skin erupted in an annoying cascade of itches and for the next five minutes, while Mr. Hunk's voice burst into song in the bathroom next door, I busied myself fighting a regular forest fire of itchiness all over my feline bod.

"Max!" suddenly a voice called out from the door.

I glanced over. It was Dooley, my best friend and wingman. Whereas I am of big-boned stock, with blorange fur, Dooley is a gray ragamuffin and considerably slighter. At the moment he was looking troubled. Now the thing you need to know about Dooley is that he always looks troubled. He is what you would call a worrier. But right now he was looking even more worried and troubled than usual.

"I know," I said. "I don't like it either."

"It's terrible!" he cried. "How long has this been going on?"

"Weeks. Months. I don't know. One day everything is fine, and then suddenly. Boom. Your life is turned upside down. It's not fair is what it is. Not fair to spring this on us."

"You've had it for months?" he asked, joining me on the bed. For some strange reason the box spring only kicks back when I try to land on it. Dooley, on the other hand, landed gracefully on all fours and gave me a look of concern. "You should have told me."

"I did tell you. I've been telling you all the time. I've done nothing *but* tell you."

"Where is it?" he asked, glancing down at the itch I was currently trying to remedy.

I gestured with my tail to the bathroom. "In there."

He glanced over, a puzzled look on his furry face. "Huh?"

"He's in there! God's gift to women is taking a shower, acting as if he owns the place, can you believe it? I swear to Sheba, Dooley, that man is moving in."

Dooley blinked. "You were talking about Chase?"

"Weren't you?"

In response, he raised his hind paw and started scratching furiously behind his right ear. "No. I. Was. Not," he said between grunts and scratches. The itch finally abated and he added, panting slightly, "I was talking about these terrible itches. These horrible, annoying itches. They started up last night and I can't seem to get rid of them."

"Itches? You have itches?"

"I have—and so do you. And so, for that matter, do Brutus and Harriet."

"That's not good."

"It's bad, Max," he said, his whiskers puckering up into an expression of extreme concern. "Do you think we caught some kind of disease? Do you think…" He swallowed visibly and lowered his voice to a whisper. "Do you think… we're going to… die?"

I groaned. "We're not going to die, Dooley. It's just an itch. It will pass."

He flapped his paws a bit. "But we all have them, Max!" His eyes widened to the size of saucers. "It's a virus! A virus that will wipe out the entire feline population!"

We'd watched a movie called *Contagion* the other night with Odelia and Chase. It was about Gwyneth Paltrow who shakes hands with a chef in Hong Kong and dies and pretty soon everyone else also dies except for her husband Matt Damon who doesn't die. It was horrible. I kept my paws in front of my eyes the entire time. Can you imagine even Kate Winslet died? After surviving that whole Titanic thing she goes and dies from some silly little virus. And now every time someone coughs Dooley thinks they are going to die, too.

"But Brutus and Harriet have it, too, and I'll bet soon every cat in Hampton Cove will have it, and then it will spread to New York and the country and the world!" He gave a hiccup and grabbed my paw, which hurt, as he neglected to retract his claws. "We're all gonna die!"

Just in that moment Chase walked in from the bathroom and we both looked up. He had a towel strapped around his private parts and was toweling his long hair. He reminded me of that movie *Tarzan* we'd seen with that vampire from *True Blood*. I know, we watch a lot of television in this house. And you thought cats didn't watch TV. Huh. Think again.

"Oh, hey, Dooley," said Chase, spotting my friend sitting next to me. Then he grinned and shook his head. "I'm doing it again. Talking to a bunch of cats. I must be going loco."

Like a pair of synchronized swimmers, both Dooley and I raised our hind paws and started scratching ourselves behind the left ears, then the right ears, then under the chin.

Chase stopped rubbing his scalp with the towel and gave us a look of concern.

"Well, what do we have here?" he muttered.

He sat down on the bed, and for some reason began inspecting me, checking my fur here and there, carefully parting my blorange hair to look at that nice pink skin underneath. Then he subjected Dooley to the same procedure. Finally, he sat back, and glanced at a smattering of red spots on his ankle and nodded knowingly. "Well, I'll be damned."

Suddenly something jumped from my neck onto the bed. Something small and black.

Quick as lightning, Chase caught it between his fingernails, and studied it for a moment, before mashing it to bits, his face taking on a serious expression. He then gave me and Dooley a long look of concern, not unlike a father about to give his daughter The Talk.

Oh, yes. I've seen movies where fathers give their daughters The Talk. But Chase wasn't my father, and I'm not his daughter, so why would he give me The Talk?

I braced myself for the worst, and judging from Dooley's claws digging into my skin, so did he.

"I hate to be the one to tell you this." Chase spoke earnestly and with surprising tenderness lacing his rumbling baritone. "But you guys got fleas."

Dooley and I shared a look of confusion. "Fleas?" I asked. "What are fleas?"

Dooley was quaking where he sat. "It's the virus! It's what killed Rose from Titanic!"

"Now, this is nothing to be concerned about," Chase continued gently, almost as if he could actually understand what Dooley was saying. "I'll tell Odelia and she'll take care of this straightaway." He patted my head again—another one of those awkward prods—and smiled. "What doesn't kill you makes you stronger. And fleas have never killed anyone. I think."

Dooley, who was on the verge of a full-scale panic attack, wailed, "We won't die?"

"Didn't you listen to the man?" I asked. "Fleas are going to make us stronger."

Another itch suddenly plagued me, and I reached with my hind paw to remedy it. But Chase beat me to the punch. He dove right in, and soon was extracting another one of those jumpy little bugs from my skin, mashing it to pieces between his fingernails.

Both Dooley and I stared at the guy like a pair of hobbits staring at Gandalf the Wizard. "He saved you, Max," said Dooley reverently. "He killed the killer bug."

"It's not a killer bug, Dooley," I said.

"He killed the killer bug with his bare hands."

"I'm telling you it's not a killer bug."

"He saved you. Chase saved you from the killer bug. He's a hero."

"It's not a killer bug and Chase is not a hero!"

But I had to admit that maybe—just maybe—I'd misjudged Odelia's boyfriend.

The man *was* a genuine hero. The fiercest fleaslayer the world had ever known.

CHAPTER 3

*B*ack at the hotel Odelia was prepared for the worst when she followed her uncle up to the second floor of the Hampton Cove Star. Downstairs, the secondary crime scene had been sealed off from prying eyes by a screen, and techies from the Suffolk County Medical Examiner's office were busily scratching their heads as they stared down at Burt's head.

Upstairs, the hotel manager, an obsequious little man with a clean-shaven face and shifty eyes, led the way to the room where the tragedy had taken place. Odelia's uncle Alec Lip, Hampton Cove's chief of police, hiked up his gun belt, while Odelia and a few more boys and girls in blue followed in the big man's wake.

As the town's prime crime reporter—or quite frankly the town's only reporter, prime, crime or otherwise—Odelia had a front-row seat to most investigations her uncle was involved in, as long as she was discreet and didn't print stuff in her paper that could hamper the investigation. A fine sleuth in her own right, she'd solved more than one crime in her time, a fact for which her uncle was more than appreciative.

"Where is Chase?" she asked now.

Her uncle cocked an eyebrow in her direction. "I should probably ask *you* that."

She blushed slightly. Chase had been living with Uncle Alec, but had been staying over at her place more and more frequently these past few weeks. She didn't know whether this was a good thing or a bad thing, but she had to admit she'd grown very fond of the cop.

"I called him," she said. "He said he'd be here."

Uncle Alec shrugged. "If he says he'll be here, he'll be here."

She glanced back at the line of cops following in her wake. They all looked away, but judging from their barely concealed smiles and pricked-up ears, they were eagerly listening in on the conversation. The whole station knew about her and Chase, and followed the budding romance with the kind of fervor usually reserved for the big Hollywood love stories.

The manager came to a full stop in front of an unremarkable door and inserted an unremarkable badge into the unremarkable slot. The mechanism gave a beep, then the door unceremoniously dropped out of its hinges and collapsed to the side, offering the stunned viewers a glance at the devastated room behind it. The place looked like a war zone.

"Oh, Lord," said the little manager, clasping his hands to his face. "Oh, dear. Oh, my."

"Not much left," said Uncle Alec gruffly, and ventured inside.

Odelia's uncle was a big man with a big belly and a big, round ruddy face. At last count he possessed three chins, two man boobs and two russet sideburns. The moment he stepped across the threshold, there was a loud creaking sound and something gave way.

One moment Uncle Alec was there—the next he was gone.

"Uncle!" Odelia cried, and took a step forward, only to be held back by the manager.

"Careful, Miss Poole, please," the man said in a breathless whisper.

They both glanced down into the chief-of-police-shaped hole at their feet. One floor down, Uncle Alec was staring up at them, looking slightly dazed and covered with chalk and debris. He was lying on a bed, which had broken his fall, an elderly lady lying next to him, clutching a sheet to her chest, and staring at him with a mixture of curiosity and surprise.

"I'm fine!" Alec called out to them, lifting an arm to indicate he was still alive. "The bed broke my fall."

Suddenly, the woman next to him said, "And my husband."

"Mh?" Alec asked.

The woman pointed to an object underneath Alec. "My husband broke your fall."

A muffled sound came from beneath the large man. "Kindly get off me, sir!"

Uncle Alec rolled from the bed, and a rumpled elderly gentleman appeared, his glasses askew. He took a few deep breaths, and proceeded to give the police chief his best scowl. "This is an outrage, sir. An outrage."

"I'm sorry," said the policeman. "And thank you."

The man was shaking his fist at the hotel manager now, visible through the hole in the ceiling. "I'm calling my travel agent, sir. This is not the kind of service I expected from this establishment! First that loud bang that woke us up and now this. Color me dissatisfied."

"You tell 'em, Earl," said his wife, still clutching the sheet to protect her modesty.

"I'm truly sorry, Mr. Assenheimer," the manager called out. "We'll comp you your room and your meals. And you can add a week to your stay. No expense."

"That's the least you can do," said the old man, slightly mollified.

Odelia stepped across the hole in the floor and carefully ventured into the room. The devastation was incredible. Walls, floor and ceiling blackened. The bed smashed against the wall. The windows blown out. In fact it was a miracle the damage had been contained to this one room. As far as she could determine—and she was no expert—the explosion must have taken place near the window, the brunt of the force directed outward.

"Maybe we should wait for the fire department, Miss Poole," said the manager.

She nodded, glancing around. Then her eyes landed on the remains of the man she'd come here to interview. His blackened and charred corpse—now conspicuously headless —had been flung onto the balcony and was now lying there, almost as if in leisurely repose. If she hadn't known better, she would have thought he was sunbathing. And had over-done it.

She narrowed her eyes. Was the man buck naked? It would appear so.

"Better step back, Odelia," her uncle's voice sounded from the door. He was scratching his chalky scalp. "This is some-thing for the experts. Not much we can do here."

He was right, of course. There was absolutely nothing they could do here.

She directed a final look at Burt Goldsmith and shook her head. Such a tragic loss. The man might not have been in the prime of his life, but he still had so much to offer.

She stepped back into the corridor and the manager heaved an audible sigh of relief. He obviously did not want more people to crash through the floor and onto other guests.

Only now did she notice that up and down the corridor doors had been opened and other hotel guests had appeared, discussing the recent events and anxiously awaiting further developments, like people do. And to her surprise she recognized several of the men who stood staring back at her. There was Curt Pigott, Most Compelling Man in the World and the man who'd put Tres Siglas beer on the map. Bobbie Hawe, Most Attractive Man in the World and face of the Quattro Siglas brew. Jasper Hanson, Most Intriguing Man in the World, representing Cinco Siglas. Nestor Greco, Most Iconic Man in the World and iconic Seis Siglas figurehead. And even Dale Parson, who'd recently been voted Sexiest Man Alive.

What was this? A convention of the Most Interesting Men in the World?

Chief Alec's people spread out and started taking down information and asking these men what they'd seen or heard. They would do the same with the other hotel guests and staff, and hopefully learn what had happened in those crucial final moments of Burt's life.

CHAPTER 4

*A*s Odelia walked out of the hotel, Chase walked in. She bumped into him and for a moment thought she'd slammed into a wall. But then the wall became animated and spoke.

"We have a problem, babe," the wall said.

And when she looked up at his usually inscrutable face, she saw genuine concern there. "What happened?" she asked.

"Check your ankles."

"My ankles?"

"Uh-huh. I checked mine so now it's your turn."

The man was not making any sense. She did as she was told, though, and lifted her pants leg to display a shapely calf and equally shapely ankle. Chase produced a sound of appreciation and his expression darkened.

"Nice," he grunted.

"Look, if this is your idea of foreplay, I've got better things to do right now. We've got a dead body upstairs." And part of it downstairs, too.

But Chase wasn't listening. Instead he'd crouched down

and was inspecting her ankle, the procedure sending a pleasant tickle up her spine. The man had the touch.

"Thought as much," he said. "They got you, too, babe."

"Who got me?"

He rose to his feet again. "The fleas."

This was the absolute last thing she'd expected. "The fleas?"

"Yup. Your cats got fleas. And they've been biting us in the ankles. The fleas, not the cats. Max or Dooley must have jumped into bed at some point during the night and left some of the little critters to feast on us, too. Fleas love to go for the ankles for some reason."

With a yelp of horror, she checked her ankles. Chase was right. The skin was dotted with red spots. Yelp! "Fleas!" she cried. "I've got fleas!"

"Not you. Your cats. I checked them before I left. They're full of the nasty little bugs."

She buried her face in her hands. "My babies got fleas! I'm officially the world's worst cat person!"

"No, you're not. No pets are safe from these pests. Probably picked them up out in the yard or got them from some neighbor cat."

She peeked between her fingers. "They all got them?"

"Yep. After I found them on Max and Dooley I went next door and Marge checked Brutus and Harriet and they got them, too." He smiled. "I feel a trip to the vet coming up."

She shook her head. "They hate going to Vena. Last time I took them they didn't stop whining for weeks."

"Yeah, well, better Vena than this flea infestation." He glanced at a couple of cops who stood interviewing hotel guests, notebooks out, pencils poised. "So what happened here? Your uncle said something about an explosion?"

The topic of the fleas dispensed with, she nodded. "Burt Goldsmith was blown up."

"The Dos Siglas guy?"

"I was just on my way to interview him when his room exploded and his head came tumbling down at my feet."

In spite of the circumstances, Chase grinned. "His head, huh?" He shook his own head. "This could only happen to you."

She whacked him on the arm. "It's not funny."

He sobered. "No, I guess it's not. So what do they think happened?"

"No idea. The room is blown to bits. Looks like a bomb went off or something."

"So no gas explosion?"

"Definitely not."

"Maybe he accidentally blew himself up?"

"Or maybe he blew himself up on purpose."

They watched as a team of Suffolk County fire marshals double-parked their big rig in front of the hotel and walked in. If anyone could find out what happened in there it was these guys. Just then, Chief Alec came walking out, wiping his brow.

"What a mess," he grumbled as he joined them on the sidewalk.

"Any leads?" asked Chase.

"Yeah, one. Kid who works room service says he brought a bottle of beer up to Goldsmith's room about fifteen minutes before the explosion. Third bottle in two days."

"Beer? You think Burt Goldsmith was killed by an exploding bottle of beer?"

Uncle Alec turned up his hands. "Who knows? Apparently there was some kind of private war going on between Burt and some of these other interesting guys. They all work for different beer companies and can't stand the sight of each other. So they like to send each other beer bottles as a taunt. These particular bottles were sent by…" He took a notebook from his pocket then groped around his head for a moment. "Where are my damn glasses?" he grumbled.

Odelia helpfully pointed to the glasses that were sticking out of his shirt front pocket.

He took them and placed them on his nose. "Thanks," he muttered, then read aloud, "A Curt Pigott. Calls himself the Most Compelling Man in the World." He removed the glasses and gave them a dubious look. "And of course Pigott claims he never sent any bottles. And definitely no exploding ones."

"He would say that, wouldn't he?" said Odelia.

"Then again, why would he use room service to kill his competitor?" Chase said. "That would be dumb."

"Good point," Alec grunted. "And if he did put some type of explosive in that bottle there would be traces on his person and in his room. Which is what we're trying to determine right now."

As they spoke, some of the interesting men came ambling out of the hotel and walked over to where Burt's remains had dropped down to the sidewalk. Burt's grandson, meanwhile, joined Odelia, Chase and her uncle. He was pale as a sheet. "This is horrible," he said. "A nightmare. What do you think happened, Chief? Is it true what they're all saying?"

"What are they saying, son?" asked Alec.

"That he did this to himself? That he committed suicide in the most spectacular way possible?" He stifled a sob. "That he went out with a bang?"

"It's too soon to tell," said Chief Alec.

"What do you think?" asked Chase.

The kid stood shaking his head, as if trying to clear it. "Grandpa would never kill himself. He loved life. He loved himself. He loved being the Most Fascinating Man in the World. I—I just can't believe it. Then again, he did love a good show." He closed his eyes, looking pained and on the verge of another collapse. "I just don't know," he said. "I just know I loved the old man to pieces and now..." He stifled another sob. "Now he is in pieces."

Uncle Alec grasped his shoulder and gave it a good squeeze. "Try not to think about it too much, son. Whatever happened here—I can promise you this: we're going to get to the bottom of it. We're going to find out what exactly happened to your grandfather and you'll be the first to know when we do."

"Thanks, Chief," said the kid hoarsely. "You're very kind."

Just then, an altercation alerted them that something was amiss. A woman came walking up to the hotel, loudly demanding to be told what was going on. She was making quite a scene, making heads turn up and down the street.

"Uh-oh," said Chief Alec.

The woman was his mother—Odelia's Grandma Muffin.

CHAPTER 5

Frankly I was having a hard time coming to terms with the tragedy that had befallen me. Fleas? Feasting on my body? The thought was too outrageous to contemplate. And yet it was true. I'd seen the little buggers, jumping up and down with joy after drinking from my blood —sticking tiny little holes in my skin with their tiny little mouths—invading the sanctity of this feline body of mine. Dooley was even more devastated by the news than me.

"Why, Max?" he was wailing after Chase had left. "Whyyyyyy?"

I could have consoled him but frankly I didn't feel up to it. And when Brutus and Harriet joined us in Odelia's back-yard, also looking glum and forlorn, the pity party was complete. Four cats, struck down by the weight of woe—or a small army of fleas.

"I can't believe it," said Harriet, the prettiest white Persian for miles around. She was licking her snowy white fur distractedly, her heart clearly not in it. "Fleas. Me. It must be some mistake."

"It's not a mistake," said her partner Brutus, a black and muscular creature who at one time had been my mortal enemy. We'd learned to coexist, though, and had struck up an awkward friendship. Well, maybe not a friendship, per se. More like a modicum of mutual respect. "Marge inspected my fur and there they were. An entire colony of bugs, snacking on this beautiful body of mine. This temple. This epitome of health and beauty. This—"

"Yes, yes, yes," I said irritably. I was not in the mood to listen to Brutus's narcissistic ramblings. Though truth be told he recited his ode to himself in a toneless voice. It was obvious he was down in the dumps with the rest of us. "Look, we can whine all we want. It's not going to do us any good! All we need to do is trust that Odelia will do the right thing."

"They lay eggs, you know," Brutus said in that same listless voice. Almost as if he hadn't heard what I said, which wouldn't be the first time. "Big giant collections of eggs. Thousands of them. Millions, maybe. And when they hatch, that'll be the end of us."

Dooley stared at him in abject horror. "Eggs!" He gulped once or twice and dropped to his paws, plunking down on the cool grass. We were seated in the shade of the tulip tree that borders Odelia's backyard. It's one of our favorite spots. Now? I wasn't so sure. Maybe these fleas had jumped from this tree onto our fur? Maybe they lived in the grass?

"Look," I said, holding up my paws. "Let's all stay calm, all right? Let's not panic."

"A colony of eggs!" Dooley cried. "On my body! Millions and millions of them!"

"I just can't with this," said Harriet, hanging her head. "This is all too much."

"I talked to Kingman," said Brutus. "And he told me fleas

can grow to be as big as mice—rats even! Can you imagine? Millions of those horrible creatures?"

"We're dead," said Dooley. "We're all dead."

"We're not dead, you guys!" I said, trying to stifle my own rising sense of panic. "Fleas don't grow to be as big as mice. Are you kidding me? If they did don't you think we would have seen them by now? Don't you think Odelia would have called an exterminator?"

"It's just like that movie," Dooley said. "First they killed Gwyneth, then they went after Rose from Titanic." He sniffed and turned over on his back, paws bonelessly flopping in the air. "Max," he bleated. "If I go first, tell Odelia about that time I broke her phone. Tell her I'm sorry. Ask her to forgive me." He snuffled. "I'll never break another one of her phones in my life. Cause I'll be dead! And dead cats don't break phones!"

"Tell her yourself," I said. "You're not going to die, Dooley. None of us are."

"I wouldn't be so sure," said Brutus. "Kingman said—"

"Oh, don't listen to that cat," I interrupted him. "He talks through his butt."

This seemed to interest Dooley. "Kingman talks through his butt? I never noticed."

"It's an expression," said Harriet. She'd stopped grooming herself and was now studying her belly—no doubt searching for that million-strong flea colony. "I don't see them," she announced. "Oh, wait. What are these little black spots? There were no black spots before." Her voice was rising sharply. "Are these eggs? Eww! EWW! Get them off! Brutus— get them OFF me!" She was patting her belly anxiously. "Brutus! BRUTUUUUUUUS!"

Brutus, always the gallant suitor, did what he could, rubbing her tummy feverishly. All the while Harriet was screaming up a storm. For a fastidious cat like herself, always looking spic and span and priding herself in her perfect grooming skills, this was nothing short of a tragedy. Imagine Kim Kardashian suddenly breaking out in hives. Only these weren't hives but some horrible bugs burrowing into our skin! Laying eggs and feasting on our blood!

"There—you missed one. Get them off! GET THEM OFF!"

Dooley watched the scene with hollow eyes. It was obvious he felt that since death was imminent, and the flea invasion inevitable, all this hullabaloo was utterly pointless. His next words confirmed this newly acquired world view. "Just let them eat you alive."

Harriet, even though in the throes of the biggest personal crisis of her life, still found the time and energy to give him a laser-eyed look that could kill. "No damn CRITTER is going to eat ME alive. I've worked too damn HARD on this gorgeous body of mine to allow ANYTHING to feast on me, least of all some LOWLY PARASITE!"

Now that was the spirit. I, for one, was a hundred percent sure Odelia would solve this mess posthaste. That's what she did. That's why I'd chosen her as my human. Oh, you may think humans choose us. Well, that's where you're wrong. Cats choose their humans, not the other way around. And I'd always prided myself in choosing the right one. She wouldn't disappoint me now. I was ninety percent sure. Maybe eighty. Definitely seventy.

Just then, Brutus drew me aside, leaving Harriet to a further inspection of every square inch of her fur and Dooley to stare up at the sky, waiting for the end to come.

"Max," he said, lowering his voice.

"Look," I said. "Kingman may be a lot of things, but he's not a critter expert, all right? So don't you believe a word that cat says. Kingman is what you might call an alarmist."

He waved an impatient paw. "Screw Kingman," he said to

my surprise. He looked agitated, and for the first time I wondered if his agitation stemmed from something other than the flea infestation. "I need to ask you a question and I need you to listen carefully."

"Sure. Shoot," I said.

"Max," he repeated, and stopped, chewing his lip.

"Uh-huh?"

He cleared his throat. "It's like this, Max..." He stared at me.

"Yes?" I said encouragingly.

He closed his eyes and rubbed his face with his paw. "Christ, this is hard."

Now he was starting to worry me. "Just tell me already, will you?"

He fixed me with a stare from between his claws. "Right. Look, you gotta promise me not to tell a soul, okay?"

"I promise."

He held up his little claw. "Pinkie promise?"

I held up my little claw and hooked it behind his. "Pinkie promise."

The suspense was killing me. What could be so important? Soon he'd scratch my paw and have me press it against his in a blood oath or something similarly ridiculous.

"I'm having issues, Max," he finally said.

"Issues?"

"Down there," he said, pointing at his tail.

"You've got tail issues?"

"Not tail issues. Pee-pee issues."

"You can't pee? You should see a urologist."

"I can pee just fine!" he growled. "It's the other thing that doesn't work."

I stared at him. "What other thing?"

He gave me an intense look.

And then I got it. The *other* thing.

"Oh. Oh!"

"Uh-huh."

"You mean…"

He nodded seriously. "It just doesn't work like it used to, Max. And now I don't know what to do."

"And I'm supposed to know?"

He gave me a hopeful look. "You're a smart cat, Max. Everybody knows that. You've been around the block once or twice or maybe even three times. Help me out, will you?"

He said it with such a pleading expression on his face that my heart melted. "Fine," I said finally. "All right. I will help you." Though for the life of me I had no idea how.

"Harriet is very unhappy," he continued. "You know she likes it rough, right?"

I pressed my paws to my ears. This I did not need to hear. "Too much information, Brutus," I said. "Just tell me what's wrong and maybe we can try and fix it."

"Well," he said, frowning, "it used to work just fine, and now it doesn't."

"What do you mean it doesn't?"

He shrugged. "The little bugger refuses to show his face."

"Maybe it's Harriet. Maybe you don't like her the way you used to."

"Oh, I like Harriet fine. She's the one for me, Max. No doubt about it."

I thought about this for a moment. "It could be a physical thing. Do you get your morning, you know, um, your morning stiffness in that general, um, area?"

He smiled proudly. "Hard as a rock, Doc."

I grimaced. "Please don't call me 'Doc.' I am not a licensed physician."

I suddenly noticed he'd dropped down on his butt and was sticking out a certain part of his anatomy and glancing at me invitingly.

"What are you doing?" I asked.

"Aren't you going to inspect me?"

In Harriet's words: eww! "No, I am not going to inspect you."

"But how else are you going to know what's wrong down there?"

"You know what, Brutus? I think we better leave this to Vena."

"No!" he cried, then lowered his voice when Harriet and Dooley glanced over. "No can do, Doc. Vena will tell Odelia and Odelia will tell everyone else and Harriet will find out and..." He closed his eyes. "When Harriet finds out my life is officially over, all right?"

"But why? If she loves you—"

He opened his eyes and hissed, "Harriet loves the butch Brutus. The he-cat. Brutus the brute. She doesn't love the sissy cat who can't get his machinery to work as it should."

"I think you're selling yourself short, Brutus. These are new and exciting times. These days lady cats love a tomcat who shows his feelings—who's not afraid to open his heart. To lay it all out there for everyone to see. It's the millennial cat they want. The soft cat. The cat who dares to cry in front of his lady cat. Shed a few tears and admit that we're all feline."

A strange sound attracted our attention. When we turned in the direction of the sound we discovered that Dooley was softly weeping, tears trickling down his furry face.

"Oh, stop crying, Dooley," Harriet said gruffly. "Are you a man or a mouse? Have you seen Brutus cry? No, you haven't. Because my Brutus is a real cat. A cat's cat. A cat who wouldn't be seen DEAD crying like a sniveling whiny little cry-baby." She directed a loving look at Brutus. "Tough as nails he is," she added proudly. "And that's what I love about him."

Brutus slowly turned back to me and raised a single whisker.

I nodded. "You're in a heap of trouble, my friend," I said.

"I told you, Doc. If you don't fix my plumbing I'm a dead cat."

CHAPTER 6

*G*randma Muffin came walking up to the small gathering in front of the hotel, shaking her fist and crying, "Where is he? Where is my lover? Don't tell me he's dead!"

Odelia and Chase shared a look of confusion. "Her lover?" asked Chase.

"She's finally lost her final marble," said Uncle Alec. He stepped forward. "Ma. What the hell do you think you're doing, making a spectacle of yourself like that?"

The old lady stood her ground. "I've come here to meet my lover. Where are you hiding him?"

Alec gave her a weary look. "And who would this lover of yours be?"

"Why Burt Goldsmith, of course. Most Fascinating Man in the World."

"Ma, Burt Goldsmith is not your lover."

She waved that fist again. "Watch your tone, son. Burt Goldsmith was my lover long before you were born."

A look of confusion stole over Alec's face. "Long before I was born?"

34

"Sure! Each time he came to town we went at it like rabbits! Burt was my lover in the swinging sixties! The time of anything goes. Not like nowadays, when people clench their butt cheeks each time someone mentions the word sex." She glanced around at the gathering crowd. "Sex!" she cried. "See how they cringe? Sex! That's right—I like sex!"

"Ma!" Alec growled, and took a firm grip on her arm and led her away and into the hotel vestibule. Odelia and Chase followed, and so did Philippe Goldsmith, who seemed to have developed an odd and rapturous fascination with the old lady all of a sudden.

Inside the hotel, Alec pushed his mother down on one of the plush sofas and towered over her. Not that it intimidated the old lady one bit. Vesta Muffin was a tough old broad, and in spite of the fact that she was rail-thin and the spitting image of Estelle Getty, with her close-cropped white hair and large glasses, she was afraid of no one—not even her son the big police chief. She pointed a bony finger in his face. "I demand to see my lover!"

"Your lover is dead," Uncle Alec said before he could stop himself.

She gasped—a quick intake of breath. "Dead?"

"Yeah, he was killed this morning."

Her face turned into a scowl. "You killed him, didn't you?"

"What?!"

"You didn't want your mother to carry on with the Most Fascinating Man in the World so you killed him before we had the chance to hold our hot and steamy reunion!"

Uncle Alec directed his eyes heavenward and planted his fists on his hips. "God, give me strength," he muttered. "Give me the strength not to strangle my own mother."

Odelia decided to step in and prevent a second murder from taking place. She took a seat next to her grandmother and held her hand. "I'm very sorry for your loss, Grandma," she said. "But I can assure you Uncle Alec had nothing to do with Mr. Goldsmith's death."

"Then who did?"

"We don't know yet. All we know is that there was an explosion in his room and as a consequence of the blast he died."

"Can I at least see the body?"

Odelia shared a quick look with her uncle, who shook his head, No!

"I don't think that's such a good idea. The explosion—it did a lot of damage."

Grandma nodded firmly, then bit her lower lip. "Just my rotten luck. To find my lover again after all these years only to have him snatched away from me—just like the first time."

"Is it really true you and my grandfather had an affair?" asked Philippe Goldsmith. He'd been listening intently and now joined the conversation.

Grandma directed a scathing look at him. "Who are you?"

"This is Philippe Goldsmith," said Odelia. "Burt's grandson."

Grandma studied the bespectacled young man with interest. "You don't look like Burt."

"I take after my mother," said the kid. "She was a dainty, delicate woman."

"I'll bet she was."

"So is it true about you and Grandpa?"

"Sure it's true—don't you believe the naysayers," she added, giving her son a nasty look. "Burt and I really whooped it up back in the swinging sixties. We were hot to trot and that's exactly what we did for all those summers he spent down here in Hampton Cove."

Philippe nodded. "Grandpa did mention that he had fond memories of this town. Which is why he was so happy to be back. Did he grow up here?"

"Nah. He was a city boy. But every summer his folks would come down to Hampton Cove and rent the old Mason place near Devil's Point. The house is long gone now, bulldozed in the eighties and developed into a big fancy hotel. Oh, the fun times me and Burt used to have. Then one summer his folks didn't come down, and I never saw him again. We didn't have no internet back then, and he never gave me his address or else I would have written. He did have my address, though, and for three years I hoped he'd write." She pressed her lips together. "He never did, so I finally mended my broken heart and moved on with my life. That's when I met Jack. He was a sailor." She shrugged. "The rest is history."

Uncle Alec grumbled something. He was part of that history, Jack being his dad.

"So how did you finally reconnect?" asked Philippe.

"He left a message on my Facebook page," said Grandma.

They all looked at her. "You have a Facebook page?" asked Odelia.

"Sure I do. No thanks to you people. I had to set it up all by myself."

"What do you need a Facebook page for?" asked Uncle Alec.

"Where else am I going to meet some nice boys?"

Alec raised his eyes to the ceiling again. "Why do you need to meet nice boys?"

"You may not want to hear this but a girl's got needs," she snapped. "And since all the nice boys are taken or on the Facebook I made myself a page. With some help from Dick Bernstein and Rock Horowitz from the senior center. They were only too happy to oblige."

Alec pinched the bridge of his nose and muttered something. It sounded like a prayer.

"Grandpa told me he met a woman online," said Philippe.

Grandma tapped her chest. "I'm that woman, kiddo."

"So he reached out to you?" asked Odelia.

"He sure did. Said he remembered me fondly and wanted to apologize about never writing to me back in the day. Turns out his folks discovered he'd been seeing some local hussy—that's me," she added proudly, "and wanted to break up the affair before things got serious. He did write me, he said, but his parents intercepted his letters and burned them."

"Just like *The Notebook*," said Chase quietly.

"I was supposed to meet him here today," Grandma continued. "For our grand reunion. And now you tell me he's dead!"

"At least in *The Notebook* they were together at the end," Odelia said.

Philippe wiped away a tear. "What an amazing story."

"Yeah, pretty swell, huh?" said Gran. She smacked her lips. "Burt promised me apple pie. Do you think he ordered and paid in advance? I could use a piece of warm apple pie."

Just then, another elderly lady stomped into the hotel lobby. Odelia recognized her as Scarlett Canyon. She was Gran's age but looked years younger. The Hampton Cove scuttlebutt had it that Scarlett had had work done on her face, which looked suspiciously wrinkle-free. It lent her an unnatural look, her lips puffy and her eyes cat-like. She also had an impressive décolletage that she liked to play up by wearing dresses a few sizes too small.

"Vesta Muffin!" she roared the moment she walked in. "You whore!"

Grandma shot to her feet. "Look who's talking!" she retorted furiously.

"Who's this now?" Chase asked.

"Scarlett Canyon," Odelia said. "She hates Gran's guts. And vice versa."

Rumor also had it that Scarlett had once tried to seduce

Gran's husband Jack and succeeded. The couple had stayed together but Gran had never forgiven either Scarlett, her former best friend, or her husband, who'd proceeded to drink himself into an early grave. The drinking had nothing to do with Scarlett, though. The man had been a closet alcoholic.

"Burt was my lover!" Scarlett cried, waving her arms dramatically. "Not yours!"

"Is it just me or does she remind you of Elizabeth Taylor?" asked Chase.

"Tell her. You'll make her day," Odelia said.

"Burt was mine—all mine!" Gran returned.

Philippe was staring from one old lady to the other, visibly confused that the scene had so abruptly switched from *The Notebook* to an episode of *Feud*.

"He always told me he loved me more," claimed Scarlett.

"That was before he met me," said Grandma.

"Impossible! Burt liked a woman with curves! Not a bag of bones."

"Burt liked women—not *skanks* who prey on other women's husbands."

"Oh, boy," said Chase. "Maybe we should break this up."

"Maybe you're right. Before these ladies break the internet." She gestured to several people filming the scene with their smartphones. Everybody likes free entertainment.

But before Chase could intervene, Scarlett broke down in tears, swooping down on one of the sofas and tremulously declaring, "My lover is dead. Now my life is over."

Philippe, who'd been following the interaction with breathless anticipation, suddenly asked, "So who of you is my grandmother?"

Both ladies looked up in confusion. "Huh?" asked Scarlett eloquently.

The kid was wringing his hands, his face flushed. "My dad

always told me his mother was a woman Burt had loved and lost in the Hamptons. So one of you must be her."

"I was wrong," said Chase. "This isn't *The Notebook*. This is *The Bold and the Beautiful*."

And to add credence to his claim, suddenly Gran cried out, "Me! I'm your grandmother, my sweet, dear boy. It's me!"

Philippe's face cleared and he opened his arms to hug his newfound relative.

Uncle Alec appeared confused. "How can you be his grandmother? Wouldn't you remember giving birth to a second son?"

Gran shrugged. "You try to remember everything that happened to you when you're my age."

"Don't you believe her! Vesta is not your grandmother!" suddenly cried Scarlett, rearing up from the sofa like an opera star and approaching Philippe. "My precious boy. You finally found me." She then threw out her hands and without warning clutched the kid to her ample chest. "My lovely, beautiful boy! My precious, precious grandson! My beloved Pierre!"

"Philippe," the kid managed from between the massive mammaries.

"Whatever."

Uncle Alec blew out a sigh. "Oh, boy."

CHAPTER 7

*D*ooley and I were wandering along the street. It had been tough to get Dooley to relinquish his spot on the ground and return animation to his listless form but finally I'd managed. I'd told him Kingman, whose owner runs the General Store on Main Street, was the town's expert on fleas, and that if anyone would know how to fight this infestation it was him.

"Do you really think Kingman can help us?" Dooley asked for the umpteenth time.

"Yes, I really think Kingman can help us," I replied. In actual fact Kingman couldn't save us if his life depended on it. But I had to get away from Harriet and Brutus who were the perfect double act to lead me straight into a nervous breakdown. As if the fleas weren't bad enough, now I had to cure Brutus's performance anxiety? Give me a break.

So a nice walk was exactly what the doctor ordered.

Soon I felt my mood lift. The slight breeze ruffling my furry flanks. The sun casting its golden rays upon a near picture-perfect world. Sidewalks full of happy people pushing strollers. Kids gurgling cheerfully. Moms merrily gossiping about other moms. I even liked the sight of all the dogs that pranced around, restrained by those nice sturdy leashes and collars.

That's how you can tell the difference between a dog and a cat: a cat will never allow a human to put a collar or a leash on them. Cats are free-roaming spirits, not slaves like dogs.

"Don't you worry about a thing," I told Dooley. "Odelia will fix this."

"I thought Kingman would fix this?"

"Someone will fix this," I said, my confidence in the happy solution returning.

"I wonder who patient zero is."

"Patient zero?"

"Don't you remember from the movie? Gwyneth was patient zero. She got the virus from bat and pig poop after she shook hands with the chef who hadn't washed his hands."

"I don't think it was bat and pig poop, exactly."

"It was some creature's poop." He turned to me, his tail swishing excitedly. "We need to find our patient zero so we can save the world."

"Maybe we should focus on saving ourselves."

"It's too late for us, Max. Even Rose from *Titanic* didn't make it."

"Oh, will you please forget about Rose from *Titanic*! It was just a movie!"

He didn't speak for a moment, then said somberly, "I'll bet I'm Rose. And I'll bet you're Morpheus from *The Matrix* and you get to live. Or maybe you're Matt Damon."

"I'm not Matt Damon and you're not Rose! It's fleas, Dooley. Stupid fleas!"

"It's an infestation," he said stubbornly. "And we saw that movie for a reason."

"Not everything happens for a reason, Dooley."

"Everything happens for a reason."

"Not everything."

"Everything."

"Oh, God!"

We walked on in silence for a moment. My happy mood dampened, I suddenly wished that instead of *Contagion* we'd seen *Ratatouille*. It was also about a group of critters but these critters lived in Paris and they could cook. I was pretty sure Dooley's outlook would improve if I could convince him fleas were happy little critters who enjoyed cooking.

We'd arrived downtown and were walking along Main Street, with its throngs of shoppers, honking cars and busy shops, when we noticed a peculiar scene. The hotel across the street from Kingman's General Store had one of its windows blown out, as if a fire had raged through it. And down on the sidewalk a sort of tent had been put up, with funny-looking people in white coveralls hovering about. They looked like astronauts.

"What's going on over there?" I asked.

Dooley barely glanced up. "Who cares?" he said. "We're all going to be dead soon."

"Nice attitude."

"It's true. Nothing Kingman or anyone else can do about it."

"Shall I tell you something that will cheer you up?"

He shrugged. "Nothing can cheer me up."

"Do you want to know what Brutus told me in confidence?"

He sighed. "What?"

"He's having trouble with his cathood."

Dooley frowned. "Trouble with…"

"His machinery."

He gave me a blank look and I could see I would have to spell this out.

"His pee-pee has stopped working."

He blinked. "He can't go wee-wee anymore?"

"I suppose he can—it's the other thing he can't do anymore."

"What other thing?"

"Sex, Dooley. Brutus can't have sex anymore."

His lips formed a perfect O, and for the first time since the fateful discovery of the flea issue, a smile slowly crept up his face, until he was softly chuckling. Dooley has never liked Brutus very much, mainly because he's had a lifelong infatuation with Harriet. So when Brutus swept in and swept the prissy Persian off her paws, it didn't endear him to Dooley.

"Brutus can't get it up?" he chuckled.

"That seems to be the gist of it."

"And I thought we were screwed."

"The best part is that he's asked me to help him."

Now he was laughing outright. "You told him no, right?"

"Oh, no, I told him I would help him. Why wouldn't I?"

He abruptly stopped laughing. "You're going to help him?"

"Of course. He's a fellow feline. I believe in helping out my fellow feline."

"Very noble of you, Max," he said, a scowl returning to his face.

"He'd do the same for me."

"I'm sure he would."

"He's not a bad cat, you know."

"Oh, he's a real prince."

I sighed. Dooley really was insufferable today. I decided to let it go.

We'd arrived at the General Store and I saw that Kingman wasn't occupying his usual perch on the checkout counter inside the store but instead sat holding court outside. And just like his owner, he seemed awfully interested in the happenings across the street.

"Hey, Max, Dooley," he said, never taking his eyes off the Hampton Cove Star.

"We need your advice, Kingman," I said by way of greeting.

Before he could respond, Kingman suddenly broke into a strange breakdancing movement, his body shivering and convulsing while he tried to scratch a spot on his lower back. I could have told him this was impossible. There are spots even the most agile of cats simply cannot reach, and Kingman, an impressively fat piebald, was never the most agile of cats, even in his prime. He finally seemed to realize this and resorted to applying his tongue to the area, licking up a storm. Finally he gave up and said in a low voice, "Stupid critters."

And then I got it. Kingman had fleas!

"Oh, no," said Dooley, who'd come to the same conclusion. "Kingman!"

"Yeah, I got 'em. Everybody's got 'em."

In that moment, as if to confirm his words, both Dooley and I broke into an equally spastic version of the flea breakdance. When Kingman raised an eyebrow, I confirmed the sad news. "We got 'em, too."

"Sure you do. Like I said, everybody's got 'em. Every single cat in Hampton Cove. From the hoity-toity to the lowliest street cats, they're all doing the flea dance today."

"But how?" asked Dooley. "Where? I mean, who is patient zero?"

Kingman frowned. "Huh? What are you talking about?"

"The first one to get the fleas," I explained. "He or she must have infected the others."

"Who cares! We got 'em. Now we gotta get rid of 'em!" He leaned in. "Little piece of advice. Free of charge. Whatever you do, don't tell your human. *Never* tell your human."

We also leaned in, Dooley pricking up his ears, his eyes wide. "Why?" he asked.

Kingman slowly raised his paw, equally slowly extended a single claw, and tapped a strange contraption located around his neck.

It was... a collar!

Dooley and I both gasped.

I hadn't seen the collar until now, buried as it was between Kingman's multiple layers of skin and flab and hidden beneath his bristly white-and-black fur.

Kingman gave us a sad nod. "Take a good look, fellas. This is what happens when you tell your human you got fleas. They put the collar on you!"

I stared at the thing in abject horror.

"But-but-but collars are for dogs!" Dooley cried. "Not cats —never cats!"

"Until we get fleas," growled Kingman. "So don't be like me, boys. No matter how much it itches. No matter how much they bite. Don't scratch yourselves in front of your human. They *will* inspect you. They *will* discover the fleas. And they *will* give you the collar." He shook his head. "You can't imagine the humiliation. The howls of derision I get from every single canine that passes my store. Laughing in my face. Calling me names. Let me tell you—better to grin and bear those damn fleas than to be subjected to this—this agony!"

Dooley gasped, and turned to me. Our eyes met and I could see my own terror reflected in his widening pupils.

Chase knew.

Chase would tell Odelia.

Odelia would take us to Vena.

And Vena would give us the collar!

Dooley was right. We were dead. Dead!

CHAPTER 8

While Grandma and her nemesis Scarlett Canyon fought over the affections of Philippe Goldsmith, Odelia decided to drop by the house. Her uncle would deal with Gran and the fallout of this Goldsmith business. Chase would deal with the police investigation into the death of the old man. But no one would deal with perhaps the more urgent business of four cats left to their own devices and suffering from a painful attack of fleas.

She walked out of the hotel lobby and out into the street, her phone pressed to her ear. Vena picked up within seconds and when she explained about her felines' predicament, the veterinarian was only too happy to squeeze her in between her other appointments.

"I don't mind telling you it's been one hell of a morning, darling," said Vena. "It's almost as if the entire cat population of Hampton Cove has been infested with this pest overnight. I'm almost out of drops and it's not even noon yet! But drop by with your cats and we'll get rid of those pests ASAP!"

As she was talking to Vena, Odelia's eyes drifted across the street and who would she see but the very cats she was discussing! They were gabbing with Kingman, Wilbur Vickery's chubby piebald, and judging from the expression on Dooley's face the conversation had just turned deadly serious.

After assuring Vena she would be there within the half hour, she quickly crossed the street and joined her two felines.

"Hey babes," she said as she crouched down next to Max and Dooley and tickled their necks. "I heard what happened. Are you in a lot of pain?"

Max gave her a hesitant look—not the kind of look he usually directed at her. Almost as if he were... afraid of her. Hard to believe, of course. She was the kind of pet owner who was adored by her pets. Always doing what was best for her little darlings—giving them the best chow on the market —allowing them to sleep at the foot of the bed—giving them cuddles and lavishing all her attention on them at every possible occasion.

"It's not that it's painful, Odelia," said Dooley with a shaky voice, as if he'd just learned a terrible truth. "It's that it's so incredibly itchy."

And to demonstrate the truthfulness of his words, he broke into a complicated set of movements, scratching pretty much every surface of his body that he could reach with his hind paws and applying tongue and teeth to the rest.

"Oh, you poor darlings," she said, getting up. "Let's go, shall we? I made an appointment with Vena. She's waiting."

Max and Dooley's eyes turned to Kingman, who gave them an 'I told you so' look and then shook his head sadly, returning indoors. She now saw he was wearing a flea collar. So he had caught the affliction, too. If what Vena said was true, every local cat had. She wondered what had started the infestation. Who, in other words, was Hampton Cove's patient zero? Probably some street cat like Clarice, who liked to roam the streets and snack from garbage dumps all across town.

"Do we have to go to Vena, Odelia?" asked Max.

"Yes, you do. You don't want to suffer these fleas forever, do you?"

"Maybe they'll, you know, get tired of me and jump ship?"

"No, they won't. They'll lay eggs and more fleas will come and you'll never get rid of them."

He slumped and she decided to cut all this back-and-forth short and picked both him and Dooley up. People were already stopping and staring at the crazy lady talking to her cats. She knew the Poole women had a reputation in town for being cat ladies, and she didn't want to make it worse by becoming a public display of crazy. Although her grandmother probably cornered the market in that particular area.

She carried both cats to her beat-up old pickup, which she'd parked in front of her dad's office, and deposited them inside.

They looked remarkably glum, which was only natural, of course. Poor darlings.

She got behind the wheel, managed to make the car's engine cough and purr, and navigated the old thing into traffic. "Are Brutus and Harriet at the house?" she asked.

Max and Dooley both nodded automatically, still looking sandbagged.

"Don't worry, you guys," she said in an attempt to cheer them up. "Vena will get rid of these pests in no time. You'll see. She told me she's seen half of Hampton Cove's cat population already and she's expecting the other half this afternoon. It would seem everyone and his tabby has caught this affliction today."

"What were you doing at the hotel?" asked Max, showing the first signs of animation since she'd picked him up at Vickery's store.

NIC SAINT

"I was going to tell you about that. Do you remember those beer commercials? The Most Fascinating Man in the World ones?"

"The old bearded man with his funny stories and the two pretty ladies?"

"That's the one. His name is Burt Goldsmith, and I was going to interview him this morning. Only turns out he got blown up."

Max did a double take. "Blown up?"

"Yeah, his hotel room exploded and he along with it."

"Maybe he was filming one of his commercials and something went wrong?"

"I don't think so. Either he killed himself—by accident or on purpose—or..." Her expression turned grim and she clutched the steering wheel a little firmer. "He was killed."

"Do you want us to snoop around?" asked Max.

"If you could, that would be wonderful," she said.

Her cats were her secret weapon as a reporter. They gave her the kinds of scoops other journos could only dream of. And since they were plugged into the local feline network, they collected stories that were pure gold once they made it into print.

"Odelia?" asked Dooley, speaking up for the first time since he got into the car.

"Uh-huh?" she said as she turned down the street where she lived.

"Are we going to die?"

She glanced in the rearview mirror. "Oh, Dooley. Of course you're not going to die. It's fleas—not cancer. By this time tomorrow you'll have forgotten about the whole thing."

"But—remember the movie the other night? Where Rose from *Titanic* died?"

Max heaved an annoyed grunt. "Not Rose from *Titanic* again, Dooley!"

50

"Rose from *Titanic* died," Dooley insisted stubbornly, "and so did Gwyneth and a whole bunch of other nice people, except for Matt Damon for some reason. And until they discovered patient zero and the bat and pig poop they had no way of stopping the disease."

"This isn't the same thing," she assured him while suppressing a smile. Dooley had a flair for the dramatic, and for some reason always thought he was going to die. "It's fleas, not some terrible virus. And you know that wasn't Rose from *Titanic*, right? Kate Winslet is an actress. She simply played a part. She's alive and well and probably still living in that nice English cottage from *The Holiday*." Though that was probably only true in the movie as well.

"Oh," said Dooley as he thought about this for a moment. It was obvious she'd given him food for thought.

"Odelia?" asked Max.

"Uh-huh," she said, parking the car in front of the house.

"Is Chase going to be living with us from now on?"

She'd extracted the key from the ignition and now sat poised, not expecting this particular question. At all. "Um…"

"I mean, he's been sleeping in your bed for the past four nights. And he's got his toothbrush and his toothpaste up in the cup in the bathroom and his underwear on that shelf you cleared for him in the bedroom closet, so…"

She blinked and turned to face her cats. They both looked at her expectantly.

"Um…"

"He seems nice," Dooley commented, that sandbagged look slightly waning.

"Yeah, he seems very nice," Max added. "And he killed a flea."

"Two fleas," said Dooley. "He's a hero. A flea-killing hero."

"Truth is, guys, I don't know. I like Chase. I like Chase a lot."

"And he likes you," Max offered.

"It would appear so," she said with a laugh. "It's just that… we're taking things one step at a time. I wish I could tell you what the future will bring, but I can't. You see, human relationships are like puzzles. Sometimes you know all the pieces will fit from the moment you dump those pieces out on the table. Other times? You just don't know. Maybe things look good for a while, and then suddenly you discover the puzzle company decided to short you a piece and without it you can't complete the puzzle. Other times you get bored laying that puzzle halfway through or things are just too hard and complicated and you give up."

Max and Dooley were frowning seriously. The puzzle analogy probably wasn't the best one she could have come up with, but there was some truth to it. She liked Chase, and she liked the way he made her feel. But it was early days, and she had no idea if he was a keeper or not. And neither, probably, did he. At any rate, things were going great, and she had no intention of taking them further by making big promises or launching big ambitious plans. Plans had a way of backfiring on her. Big time. So she wasn't going to jinx anything at this point when everything was humming along fine.

She gave them both a poke in the tummy. "You guys sit tight and I'll pick up Harriet and Brutus, okay?"

As she slammed the door, Max and Dooley were still brooding. She smiled to herself. Sometimes, she thought, her cats were almost more human than most humans she knew.

And a heck of a lot smarter, too.

CHAPTER 9

$\mathcal{C}$hase and Chief Alec took a seat on one of those plush overstuffed chairs in the hotel lobby. With the fire marshals going over Burt Goldsmith's room with a fine-tooth comb, trying to figure out what exactly happened there, the techies wrapping up Burt's body and transferring it to their van, and Alec's people talking to staff and guests, they took a respite.

"Do you really think your mom had Burt Goldsmith's son?" asked Chase.

Chief Alec patted at the few remaining strands of hair on his wide dome and groaned. "I don't know what to think, buddy. You would imagine a woman would know if she popped out a second son at some point in the past."

"She says she doesn't remember. Which doesn't mean it didn't happen."

Alec gave him his best scowl. "Wipe that grin off your face, Chase. I'm begging you."

Try as he might, though, Chase could not comply. The situation was simply too outrageous. "Could be that your mother is one of those women who don't even notice they're pregnant, then pop out a newborn without paying attention and go on about their business without a second glance." At least that was the story Grandma had told them.

"I find that very hard to believe. And I find it equally hard to believe Scarlett Canyon would have the exact same story to tell. About the baby just suddenly... being there, I mean." He waved his hands about a bit. "I mean—how can a baby just... pop?! That's impossible!"

"And yet it happened, if your mother is to be believed."

The Chief groaned some more. The big man was clearly in the throes of some extreme emotion. It's not every day that a man discovers he has a secret brother who's the son of the Most Fascinating Man in the World. "You wanna know what I think?"

"I definitely do, Alec. I definitely do." Alec gave him an extremely dirty look and Chase laughed, clapping the older man on the back. "I'm sorry. It's just funny is all."

"Maybe for you it is. For me this is like a nightmare and I just can't seem to wake up."

"Tell me, big guy. What is it you think?"

Alec took a deep breath. "I think that Mom decided she wants some of those Goldsmith millions for herself, and by pretending to be Burt's son's long-lost mother, she just might get her hands on a big chunk of it."

"You dare accuse your own mother of being a gold digger?"

"As a matter of fact I do. I think Mom is sick and tired of having to ask her son-in-law for handouts and now that she saw her chance clear to topping up her bank account with a nice fresh pile of cash she's not going to let that golden opportunity slip through her fingers."

Alec had a point. Grandma Muffin liked to spend money like water. If she wasn't buying online beauty treatments she was being duped by scammer apps on the App Store and maxing out the credit cards Tex Poole kept giving her. The lady liked to live big, and since Tex had taken away those very credit cards, she wasn't happy.

"I think this whole thing will shake out just fine," Chase said, leaning back and watching the goings-on in the lobby of this fine hotel. His grandfather had stayed here, though not in Burt's room, and as his thoughts turned to the old man, a sense of well-being spread through him. He might be a simple cop in a small town, but he had big plans. And those big plans involved starting a family with a particular feisty blond-haired reporter. If only this particular reporter felt the same way about him as he felt about her.

Alec must have sensed this shift in his mental processes, for he eyed him intently.

After a moment, Chase laughed and said, "What?"

"You haven't been home a lot lately, have you?"

"No, sir, I haven't."

He'd been bunking with Alec since arriving in town, something for which he was still mighty grateful. In the process, he and the chief of police had struck up a fine friendship, and he had a feeling the older man was about to abuse that friendship by giving him a piece of advice. He didn't mind. He could use all the advice Odelia's uncle cared to dispense.

"Been sleeping over at my niece's place?"

"Yes, sir, as a matter of fact I have."

"You like that girl, don't you, son?"

He smiled widely. "You got my number, Alec. I do like your niece. In fact I don't think it's too much to say that I love her."

"Oh, bringing out the L word, huh?"

"Yes, sir. Only the L word will do for what I feel for Odelia Poole."

"Well, let me give you a piece of advice, son."

Here it came.

"The way to Odelia's heart is those damn cats of hers."

He looked up. Huh? "Say what?"

Alec poked a finger in Chase's chest for emphasis. "Shower those cats with love and affection and she'll look upon you differently. That's my piece of advice for you."

For a moment he thought the other man had lost it. "Odelia's cats."

"Max, Dooley and Harriet. Focus on those three. I don't know about Brutus. He's something of an interloper."

"Like me."

Alec didn't laugh. "Maybe you are, maybe you ain't. Too soon to tell."

He gulped a little. "But she likes me, right?"

The chief wiggled his head. "Eh. I guess she does. The thing you need to know about Odelia is that she's been through a lot, son. She's been with plenty of fellas in her time and none of them turned out the way she hoped. She's taking a mighty big leap letting you sleep over. As far as I know that's a first for her." And there was that finger again, poking his chest. Alec was leaning in now, too, his face inches from Chase's. "So don't you go and break that girl's heart now, you hear?"

"You know I won't."

"Cause if you break my favorite niece's heart, I'll break your neck, understand?"

"I thought Odelia was your only niece?" he quipped.

But Alec didn't crack a smile. The man was serious. "Promise me."

"I promise, I promise. I will not break your favorite niece's heart."

"Fine." He relaxed a little. "Now that we've got that out of the way, I don't think it's too much to say that you're by far my favorite of Odelia's many boyfriends so far."

"That's… great to hear. I guess."

Alec slung a hand around his shoulder and gave him a fatherly squeeze. "Keep this up and you might even marry into the family." Just then, Grandma Muffin came stalking through the lobby, shouting a few carefully chosen obscenities at Scarlett Canyon, who was teetering on high heels in front of her and shouting right back. "Not sure that's such a good idea, though, considering this family of mine is batshit crazy," Chief Alec added with a sigh.

CHAPTER 10

*V*ena's was bustling like never before. In fact I don't think I'd ever seen so many cats squeezed into the tiny waiting room before. All of them were glancing around morosely, and all of them were in a plaintive mood, the topic of fleas dominating every conversation. Even Shanille was there, the leader of cat choir and Father Reilly's cat. Father Reilly himself was looking glum, possibly not used to taking time out of his busy schedule to take his cat to the vet.

Since it was standing-room only, Odelia leaned against the wall, the four of us nicely bundled at her feet.

"Your cats are so well-behaved!" a woman remarked, referring to the way we were the only cats not cooped up in those plastic cage contraptions. "How *do* you manage?"

Odelia shrugged. "I tan their hides if they step out of line. Nice crack of the whip."

The woman pressed her lips together and shook her head. No sense of humor.

Odelia didn't need to 'tan our hides' to make us behave. We were so terrified to visit Vena's that we didn't stir an inch from the spot where Odelia had plunked us down. And so were the other cats. You may think that cats love going to the vet. Think again. We hate the vet. We hate to be prodded and pricked and having our gums checked and our tummies measured. It's degrading. It's humiliating. It's very anti-cat. Sure, it's supposed to be good for us. I don't care. I still hate it. Now, though, with the notion that Vena would rid us of our flea infection, I was prepared to give her the benefit of the doubt.

Not the other cats, though. They were all plaintively meowing up a storm.

Dooley, meanwhile, seemed to have other interests. He'd been brooding a lot on the drive over, and now it became clear about what. "So you said that the fact that Chase has moved in has something to do with babies, right?" he asked Harriet.

"Oh, Dooley," she said, exasperated. "Are you still going on about that?"

"What did you mean when you said that?" he insisted stubbornly.

"Isn't it obvious? When a human male and a human female move in together it's because they want to make human babies."

Dooley uttered a shocked gasp. "Odelia is having babies?"

"Of course she is. She's a human female and human females need to have babies before a certain age. Something really old, though. Probably like twenty or something."

Dooley turned to me. "How old is Odelia now?"

"No idea. Ten? Fifteen maybe?"

"That sounds about right," Brutus agreed. "Chase is probably the same age as Odelia and I'm six and I know Chase is a lot older than me so he's probably ten years old by now. Fifteen at the outside," he allowed.

"That means Odelia still has oodles of time to have

human babies," said Dooley. "Years and years and years. So why have them now?!"

"It's an urge," Harriet knew. "Humans get this inexplicable urge to make babies. I think it's very strange but there you are. Urges. They get them and Odelia is no exception."

Odelia would have commented but the other humans in the room would have looked at her strangely if suddenly she broke out into meows. So she kept her mouth shut. It was hard for her, though, judging from the scarlet blush that had crept up her cheeks. Her lips were trembling, too, and if I hadn't known any better I would have thought she was trying to keep from bursting out laughing. Which was impossible, of course, as we were having this very serious, very adult conversation right under her nose.

"She needs to control this urge," Dooley said. "She needs to know that we're her babies and she doesn't need human babies so she needs to control this urge and she needs to control this urge now, before Chase does…" He turned to Harriet again, whom he seemed to consider the expert on all things human all of a sudden. "What part does Chase play in this whole baby making thing?"

Harriet frowned. "Well, he's the one who needs to put the baby in her, obviously, so at some point he'll probably…" She flicked her eyes to Dooley and then to me. "Has Dooley ever had The Talk?"

"I'm not sure," I said. "I never gave him The Talk."

"What talk?" asked Dooley.

"The Talk," Harriet clarified.

"I don't get it," said Dooley.

Harriet sighed exaggeratedly. "Brutus. Please give Dooley The Talk."

"Why do I have to give him The Talk? Why can't you give him The Talk?"

"Because you're a male and Dooley is a male and only males should give other males The Talk. It's a rule."

"It's not a rule."

"It's a rule. I didn't invent it."

"There's no rule about that. There's no rule that says only males can give other males The Talk," Brutus protested. "In fact I think it's much better coming from you."

"Guys!" Dooley cried. "What is The Talk?!"

"Look," I said, deciding to get this over with. Like a band-aid, you just had to rip it off. "You know how a male cat and a female cat get together and a couple of months later lots of kittens come out?"

"Uh-huh."

"With humans it's the exact same thing. The male of the species and the female of the species, um, lie together, as they do, and then a couple of months later babies pop out."

"How many babies?" he asked, darting curious glances at Odelia, as if expecting a litter of babies to suddenly emerge from our human.

"Oh, I don't know," I said vaguely. "A few, probably."

"One," said Brutus. "Usually humans have the one baby."

"That's it?" I asked, frowning. "That can't be true."

"It's true. Humans are stingy. They just have the one baby."

"Sometimes they have two," Harriet said. "Or three or four. But it's rare. So rare that when humans have, like, eight babies in a single litter, they get their own TV show. It's true."

"Humans are weird," Brutus agreed.

"So… how long before these babies arrive?" asked Dooley, still staring at Odelia, who was still having trouble keeping a straight face.

"Oh, maybe like three months?" I said. "Two?"

"You guys!" Dooley said. "Odelia and Chase have been

lying together for weeks now, so these babies might pop out any moment now!" He buried his face in his hands. "Oh, no."

"Relax, Dooley," I said. "Humans don't always have babies when they lie together. They have to... do stuff."

"Yeah, and then sometimes they take a pill and then they don't have the babies," Harriet explained. She seemed to know an awful lot about this stuff. Then again, at her house they watched the Discovery Channel all the time, which was probably where she got her information.

"They take a pill?" asked Dooley, looking up. "What pill?"

"Yeah, what pill?" I asked. This was news to me, too.

Harriet shrugged, studying her fingernails. "I dunno. Some pill."

Dooley turned to me, and I could see the question in his eyes before he formulated it. "Does Odelia have this magic anti-baby pill, Max?"

Ugh. "How should I know?"

His face took on a determined look. "We need to find out. This is life or death, Max."

I was afraid to ask. "Why is this life or death, Dooley?"

"Because the moment Odelia has her babies she'll get rid of us!"

And there it was. The crux of the matter. I had to admit I'd given the matter some thought myself. Our mailwoman Bambi Wiggins recently had a baby, and her cat Ellen had told us that there are three rules for cats when in the presence of a human baby: don't scratch the baby. Don't sit on the baby. Don't bite the baby. But I could tell Ellen wasn't entirely sanguine about her position in the Wiggins household herself now that this baby was born. She tried to put on a brave face, but there's a long-held rumor amongst cats that the moment humans have babies those same humans' cats get offered a one-way ride to the pound. And if there's one place us cats fear even more than the vet, it's the pound.

"We have to stop her," Dooley whispered, loud enough for the entire waiting room to hear. "Odelia can never have babies, Max. We need to stall her until she's too old! Which is only…" He made a few quick calculations in his head. "Two more years!"

"Ten," Harriet corrected him. "She's ten now, which makes her twenty in ten."

"Fifteen at the outside," Brutus repeated. "Which gives you a window of five years."

He cut me an urgent look. I knew what that look meant: have you thought of some remedy or cure for my very delicate issue, Max? I gave him a look back that said: no, Brutus. I haven't. But I was adamant to bring it up with Vena when I had the chance, whether he liked it or not.

What? I'm not an expert on tomcat anatomy. Vena is. Which is why she gets paid the big bucks.

CHAPTER 11

*D*ooley, Brutus and Harriet were still discussing the baby thing, so I pawed Odelia's leg until she picked me up. I had an important message to deliver and now was the time to do it.

"Brutus has issues, Odelia," I told her quietly, making sure the other members of our cat menagerie couldn't overhear us.

"I'll say," she said between unmoving lips. "You guys are so funny."

I had no idea how to respond to that, so I went on, "He's having pee-pee issues."

This time a frown appeared on her brow. "Pee-pee issues?"

I cut a quick glance down to the floor, but Brutus was still engrossed in the entire pill discussion so the coast was clear. "You need to ask Vena to take a look at his pee-pee," I said. "But don't tell her I told you, cause this is a very sensitive matter for Brutus and he'll probably kill me if he found out I told you to tell Vena."

Odelia smiled. Cat drama. She knew all about it. "Fine,"

she said, her lips still not moving, her eyes darting about the room to make sure nobody saw she was talking to her cat. I didn't know how she did it. Each time I meow or mewl my lips have a tendency to part. Hard to keep them pressed together and still hold a well-enunciated conversation.

I made to jump back down but Odelia held onto me. "Wait. Tell me more about this pee-pee thing."

"What more is there to tell?"

"Does he have pain when he urinates?"

Ugh. I so didn't want to discuss this topic. "He urinates just fine. It's the other thing that doesn't work."

She frowned, confused. "What other thing?"

I cocked a knowing whisker at her. And then she got it.

"Oh!"

"Yeah."

"The... Brutus and... Harriet."

"Yup."

"You mean his soldier refuses to salute."

Gah. "I think I've heard enough," I said, and gracefully jumped down to resume my position at her feet. And it was then that the conversation really turned weird.

"Did you hear about that explosion this morning?" asked Shanille.

"Yeah, some old guy got blown up, right?" said Tom, the butcher's cat.

"Not just some old guy," said Tigger, the plumber's cat. "The Most Fascinating Man in the World. My human loves those commercials. My human loves beer," he clarified.

"Your human is a raging alcoholic," said Shanille disapprovingly.

"He is not. He loves beer, that's all. And Scotch. And vodka. And—"

"Kingman told me the guy's cat is missing," said Misty, the electrician's cat.

"The Most Fascinating Man in the World had a cat?" I asked.

"Sure he did. The Most Fascinating Cat in the World. She was in some of those commercials. What's her name again?" Misty clicked her nails annoyedly, then her face cleared. "That's right. Shadow. Great name for a cat, huh?"

Shadow, who belongs to Franklin Beaver, the guy who runs the hardware store, grinned. "I like it."

"I think he likes gin, too," said Tigger, frowning, "though I'm not sure. He definitely likes his Martinis. Neat, not stirred or shaken. Poured straight from the bottle."

"Maybe we should talk to this Shadow, Max," Dooley suggested. "Find out what he knows."

"Shadow is a she," said Misty. "Not a he. At least that's what Kingman told me."

"I'm not a she," said Shadow, a shadow passing over his face. "I'm a he."

"Well, she's a she," said Misty decidedly. "So there."

"And he likes his brandy, too," said Tigger musingly. "Pear brandy, if I'm not mistaken. And apple." He shrugged. "He's not picky. Very happy-go-lucky guy, my human. Very easy."

I held up my paws. "Where can we find this Shadow—he or she?"

Misty frowned. "Like I said, Kingman thinks Shadow went missing. Right after the explosion."

"Must have scared the living daylights out of her," Shanille agreed. "I know I wouldn't enjoy my human being blown up." She darted a quick look at Father Reilly, ascertaining he was still there, and had not been blown up while she wasn't looking.

"None of us would enjoy our humans being blown up," I said.

"Speak for yourself," a ratty little cat piped up. I recognized her as the landscaper's tabby. "Wanna know what my human did? Accidentally stuck me in the washer. The washer! I wanted to have a look-see and the doofus closed the door on me! It's a miracle I survived!"

We all stared at the cat. She looked a little worse for wear but very much alive.

She sighed. "At least I don't got fleas, like you lot do." She scratched a floppy left ear. "It's this damn water in my ears that bugs me, though. Can't get it out! Soapy water. Ugh."

"And then there's wine, of course," said Tigger, his face clearing. "Oh, he loves his wines. He loves his red wines, he loves his white wines, he loves his rosés—"

"Will you shut up already?" asked Shanille plaintively. "I don't care about your alcoholic human's addictions and disgusting predilections."

"Practice some kindness, Shanille," Tigger said, stung. "Isn't that what your human teaches? Kindness and your basic Christian compassion?"

Shanille tilted her chin. "I'll have you know I don't go in for all that religious stuff."

"Your human runs a church for a living!"

"So? Your human unclogs toilets for a living. That doesn't mean you have to."

"It's not the same thing and you know it."

Pretty soon the whole thing erupted into a war of words, as it often does when a bunch of cats get together. I decided to do the smart thing and stay out of it. Instead, I turned to my compatriots, who sat following the back-and-forth with glittering eyes and clicking claws. Oh, cats do love a good cat fight. "You guys, we have to find this cat Shadow. Maybe she saw what happened to her human." I looked up at Odelia who gave me a wink.

"Sure, sure," said Brutus, who seemed eager to jump into the fray.

I sighed. "Harriet?"

"Shush, Max," the Persian said. "I think Shanille is about to implode."

I turned to my wingman. "Dooley?"

"I'll help you, Max," he said. "On one condition."

"What?"

"That you'll help me find Odelia's magic pills."

And we were right back where we started.

Moments later we were finally called into Vena's consultation room for our big inspection. I'll spare you the details, but none of us came out unscathed that day. She applied some kind of weird-smelling gel to our necks, then handed Odelia an equally weird-looking comb with the advice to use it at least twice daily with a little soapy water, and finally gave our human the option to apply the dreadful collar or not.

"Quite frankly I'm using them less and less," said Vena. "I find that they produce a horrible rash or allergic reaction in some cats, while others get them snagged on tree branches and such, which is potentially dangerous, as you can imagine. Still others lick them and end up with a severe reaction from the poison. So what shall it be? You decide, Odelia."

All four of us looked up at Odelia, begging her to say no to the collar.

She gave us her sweetest smile, then proceeded to say yes to the collar.

CHAPTER 12

$\mathcal{O}$delia stepped into her dad's office. As usual, the outer office was filled with people waiting for their doctor's appointment. The one thing missing, though, was Grandma, who usually sat at her perch behind the reception desk, directing traffic, taking calls, jotting down appointments and gossiping with her son-in-law's patients.

Odelia nodded hello to the familiar faces, then glanced at the empty counter. No Gran. Odd. She'd wanted to have another word with her relative about this whole Burt Goldsmith business. Talk some sense into her. And now she hadn't even shown up for work. Not that she needed the job. She'd practically begged Dad to give it to her. Said she'd go crazy sitting at home doing nothing. Said she'd be the best receptionist he'd ever wished for.

Dad had relented and she'd been the worst receptionist he'd ever wished for.

And Odelia was just about to turn away when the door to the inner office opened and her dad appeared, along with Mrs. Baumgartner, one of his regulars. The bluff middle-aged woman thanked him and went on her way. Dad's eyes scanned the waiting room, then the empty desk, and he sighed. When he caught sight of his daughter, he visibly perked up. "Odelia, honey. Come on in." He turned to the other patients. "We'll just be a moment."

"Take your time, Doctor Tex," said an elderly man with beetling brows and a stoop. "We're not going anywhere."

"Speak for yourself, you old fool," said his neighbor, a squat ruddy-faced woman.

"One minute," Tex promised, and ushered Odelia into his exam room.

"You don't look so hot, Dad," she said, noticing his pale and sweaty brow and his unkempt mop of white hair. Even his doctor's coat had been buttoned askance. She set about to remedy this and her father took the opportunity to wipe his forehead with a napkin.

"It's been hell all morning," he confessed. "Between the patients and the phone calls I don't know what to do first. Where the hell is your grandmother? I've tried calling but she keeps blocking me. I didn't even know she could do that on that crappy phone I gave her."

Grandma used to have a snazzy iPhone, but kept buying expensive apps in the App Store. And then she broke her phone by dropping it in the toilet. So now Dad had bought her a cheaper model. Some unknown Chinese brand. And Gran hadn't answered his calls since.

"She thinks she gave birth to the son of the Most Fascinating Man in the World," Odelia said, patting her dad on the chest, his doctor's coat nice and neat once more.

"Come again?" he said.

In a few brief words she explained what had happened at the Hampton Cove Star that morning. Tex plunked himself down on the edge of his desk, looking stunned. "She *thinks* she gave birth to a third child but she's not entirely *sure*? That's crazy!"

"That's not all. Scarlett Canyon claims *she* is the mother of Burt's child. Though her memory is equally fuzzy."

"Crazy town," muttered Tex, wiping his brow once more. "Is that why she didn't show up for work this morning?"

"Yeah, she had a hot date with Burt."

"She could have told me."

"You haven't exactly been on speaking terms, Dad."

"That's true," he admitted.

Ever since Tex took her credit cards away—or his credit cards, actually—Gran had been ghosting him. Tough to do when you work together, but Gran had managed. Slipping him little pieces of paper and talking to the wall whenever she needed to address him.

"You think she's going to quit working here?"

"If she can get Philippe Goldsmith to believe her claim she might," Odelia said. "Burt's 'widow' stands to come into a nice chunk of change, if Philippe is to be believed."

"Maybe it's for the best," said Dad, staring at the ceiling. "Maybe this Philippe is taking your grandmother off our hands and she'll live with the guy in Vegas from now on."

"Colorado."

"Colorado is fine. I can live with Colorado. Mexico would have been better. Or Africa."

"I'm not sure Mom will like her mother moving away."

Dad humorously slapped the desk. "There's always a catch, isn't there?"

"She'll be back, Dad."

"Not what I wanted to hear," he said with a grin, then pressed a kiss to her brow. "And now you better scoot, young lady. Before my patients chase you out of here, feathered and tarred."

"Maybe you should call the temp agency. At least until Gran comes to her senses."

"Maybe I should," he conceded, and walked her out.

Next stop was the library, where Odelia's mother was stacking books in neat rows onto a library cart. "Oh, hey, honey," Mom said. "Have you seen your grandmother? She was supposed to arrive early today. Help me prepare for the lecture tonight." Mom, who was the spitting image of her daughter, pressed her hands into her lower back and arched backwards, grimacing. "Ooph. My back is killing me today."

"Lecture? What lecture?"

"The Most Interesting Men in the World are in town. They're doing some type of conference thing at the Seabreeze Music Center. I managed to snag them for an Evening with the Most Interesting Men in the World. Only it looks as if it might get canceled."

"Of course. The explosion."

"Explosion? What explosion?"

For the second time she told the story of the explosion that had taken the life of the Most Fascinating Man in the World.

"Bummer," said Mom. "He was supposed to be the star of the evening. Not to mention the emcee." She bit her lip. "Maybe the others will still show up?"

"They're all being questioned as we speak, and it looks like the Most Compelling Man might be a suspect in the whole thing."

Mom nodded knowingly. "Jealousy. Figures. They don't seem to be able to agree on anything. Not the topics of conversation, not the seating arrangements or the order of introductions—not even the name of the evening. I wanted to call it 'An Evening with Some Very Interesting Men,' but they said that would favor the Most Interesting Man in the World, who, coincidentally, couldn't make it. Apparently there's a pecking order of Most Interesting Men with the Most Interesting Man numero uno and Burt Goldsmith a close second. Maybe I should call the whole thing off now. Quite frankly it's not worth the aggravation."

"You haven't heard the worst part yet," Odelia told her. "You have a second brother."

Like her father, Mom plunked down on the first solid object she found, in her case the library cart, disturbing the neatly placed books and dumping them all to the carpeted floor. "What?" she asked, pressing a hand to her heart.

As Odelia told the story, the thought occurred to her that this was almost like an episode of *The Jerry Springer Show*. "And since Gran hasn't shown up at Dad's office there's a good chance she'll be leaving us soon to go and live in Burt Goldsmith's mansion in the Centennial State, sending us postcards from time to time while she lives it up out there."

"Oh, dear," said Mom. "How did your father take it?"

She wanted to say Dad was over the moon but that seemed inappropriate. "He's concerned about you and Alec. The news of this third sibling must be tough on you guys."

Mom raised an eyebrow. "Tough? Either your grandmother has finally gone off her rocker or she's in this for the money. And if she is, the woman is dead to me."

Odelia was surprised by the resolute tone in her mother's voice. "I'm sure she'll come to her senses. She always does."

"Dead!" Mom exclaimed, getting up. "After all that we've done for her? Leaving us high and dry? She can join her newly acquired grandson in Colorado and choke!"

"Um, that seems kind of harsh, Mom."

Mom swept up an arm. "She needed support after my dad died? We gave it to her. She needed a place to stay after it turned out Dad had gambled away the house? We took her in. She wanted a job so she could stay active and earn some extra money? We gave her two jobs! And now this!"

She was now stocking the shelves with Nora Roberts books at such a rate and with such fury the entire cabinet shook. Mom was usually a soft-spoken and gentle person but now she resembled Lizzie Borden before taking up the ax and chopping down her relatives.

"I, um—do you need help? I mean, now that Gran probably won't show up?"

Mom planted a hand on her hip. "I'm sorry, honey. But it's been one of those days."

Yup. One of those days where you find out your mother secretly had a second son. Or not. "I'll just put these away, shall I?" she suggested, and pushed the cart away from her mother before she bodily lifted it up and hurled it through the large plate glass window.

And as she was collecting more returned books and stocking the shelves, she said, "Oh, I forgot to tell you but I took the cats to Vena's."

"Uh-huh," said Mom without much enthusiasm from the next aisle.

"She squirted some topical gel on their necks and gave me a flea comb."

"Mh."

"She wasn't sure about a flea collar but the poor creatures are so riddled with fleas I'm going to have them wear them for a while. Only a couple of days. Until they're free of the pests. And I'll have to vacuum the carpets, the floors, the bed, the sofa, wash the sheets…"

"That's great, honey," her mother said distractedly, probably still fuming. Odelia could hear the tack-tack-tack of books being stacked on the rack. It sounded like gunfire.

"You should probably do the same."

"Mh."

Odelia heaved a sigh. Looked like Mom was a goner for now. At least until she got what she perceived as Gran's betrayal out of her system. Which could take a while. And as she filed a Debbie Macomber Christmas novel under the letter M, she thought about what Max had said. Burt Goldsmith had a cat. A cat that had gone missing. If Max could find out where Burt's cat was holed up and talk to her, there was a lot he could find out.

She suddenly remembered the conversation about her and Chase having babies and smiled to herself. It wasn't just Mom who could get worked up. Her cats did, too. As if she and Chase were ever going to have babies. Hah. Just the thought was ridiculous.

Still, the sudden fire lighting up her core at the thought of having Chase's babies told her otherwise. She tamped down on the sudden heat. The whole thing was ridiculous. Absolutely ridiculous.

But when her phone lit up with a message from Chase she felt ridiculously excited.

CHAPTER 13

*W*e were stuck on the fire escape. No doubt about it. Staring at a closed door willing it to open and the door wasn't budging. At least not until some helpful human opened it for us. That's the disadvantage of being a cat. No opposable thumbs. Imagine the damage we could do if only our creator had outfitted us with opposable thumbs. We could actually open this damn door. Oh, wait. Human to the rescue. A young man dressed like a bellboy shoved open the door, pinned it against the wall so it stayed open, and took out a pack of cigarettes.

Dooley and I slipped inside.

Thank God for smokers.

"You know, Max?" said Dooley as we traversed the nicely carpeted corridors of the Hampton Cove Star hotel. "This collar isn't so bad. I mean, it smells like diesel fumes and everything but it's not a smell I can't get used to, if you know what I mean."

I rolled my eyes. I hated the collar from the moment Vena put it on me. Like Dooley said, it smelled like diesel, and it itched. Besides, cats aren't meant to wear collars. Dogs are.

Because dogs are an inferior species. Cats are meant to roam wild and free. Collars don't feature into that story. Odelia had promised us it was only for a few days. Until all the fleas had fled. Between the drops and the collar and the comb she said she'd apply to our furs, it wouldn't take more than two or three days for this whole terrible episode to be behind us.

"I mean, as long as it's for a good cause I'm quite willing to wear the collar," Dooley prattled on. "I'm not saying I like it. But I'm not saying I don't like it, either."

I kept a dignified silence. As long as we didn't meet A) other cats, and B) dogs, I was fine. Kingman might get away with wearing a collar and keeping his dignity, I could not.

We'd arrived at the room formerly occupied by the Most Fascinating Man in the World, now fascinating the Suffolk County medical examiner with how dead he was, and peered inside. The door was missing, but some helpful police officer had put up yellow crime scene tape to keep people out. People, not cats.

We entered the room, padding around a nice hole in the floor, and checked around for signs of Shadow, Burt Goldsmith's elusive cat.

"Shadow," I called out. "Where are you?"

"Shadow," Dooley echoed. "Here, kitty, kitty."

I gave Dooley a scowl. Cats don't debase themselves by using those awful words. Here, kitty, kitty indeed. We covered the entire hotel room in half a minute. Not much to see. Terrible smell, though. Like when Odelia burns her toast in the morning. But worse. Much worse. I thought I even smelled charred meat at some point in the proceedings. Yikes.

We got out of there as fast as we could, having exhausted our options and our capacity to take in terrible odors. Out in the corridor, a door opened and a man walked out, a cat slipping out in his wake.

"Don't be too long, Princess," said the man softly, and the cat growled something rude that the man probably didn't understand, for he heaved a contented sigh and giggled.

The door closed and the cat stared at us. We stared back. It was one of those Clint Eastwood moments, from the days when Clint still starred in westerns as the inscrutable hero with the inscrutable squint. Then the cat spoke. "What are you doing here?"

"I'm glad you asked," said Dooley, approaching the black cat. He wasn't just black but more as if a black hole had suddenly opened up in the corridor floor, only the whites of his eyes indicating he was animated by the force of life. That and that grating voice. "We're looking for Shadow? The Most Fascinating Cat in the World? Maybe you've seen her?"

The black cat—Princess, according to his owner—merely continued to stare.

"We're trying to figure out what happened to Shadow's human," I explained. "Apparently he was blown up this morning and we're trying to determine if foul play was involved."

"You fools," Princess growled. "Of course foul play was involved. What do you think? That he accidentally blew himself up when he lit a cigar? The guy was murdered!"

"Oh," said Dooley excitedly. "Do you have any evidence to corroborate this theory, my friend?"

The cat growled something between gritted teeth, looking and sounding just like Clint, Clint squint and all. For a moment I fully expected him to snarl, 'Make my day, punk.' Instead, he said, "Corroborate? What are you? Some two-bit Sherlock Holmes wannabes?"

"We work with Odelia Poole," Dooley explained helpfully. "She's an investigator and a reporter. She helps out the police from time to time when they're stuck. She's very smart."

"Yeah, right. A bunch of loser cats helping a nosy parker journo solve crime. Where have I heard that before?"

"I'm sorry," I said. "But did I hear your owner call you Princess?"

"That's my name, don't wear it out," he growled.

"But... isn't Princess a female name?"

"I am a female," he snarled. "Can't you tell?"

Frankly I couldn't, but I was prepared to be broad-minded. "So, Princess, can you tell us some more about this theory of yours? Burt Goldsmith was murdered, you say?"

He—or she—was reluctant, I could tell, but finally the desire to confide in someone won out. "Someone was after him, all right. Shadow used to say they were all after Burt."

"All?"

"All the interesting men. His competitors. All except one, of course. The Most Compelling Man in the World. My human." She stuck out her chest. "Curt wouldn't hurt a fly. He's the greatest. And the most compelling, of course."

"Of course," I said graciously.

"You look like a male," Dooley said abruptly. He'd been studying the black cat closely.

"I was born a male," Princess explained gruffly. "But then I decided I was a female. What's it to you, you insensitive bozo?"

"Just curious, I guess," said Dooley, not insulted in the least.

"I always felt like a female trapped inside a male body. Do you have any idea what that does to a cat? No, of course you don't, you ignoramus. Well, take your judgments and shove them up your keister, will you?"

"What's a keister?" asked Dooley, interested.

"Never mind," I said, intent on steering the conversation back to safer ground. "Do you have any idea where we can find Shadow? We'd like to ask her some questions."

"If they're as dumb as the ones you've been asking me I don't know if I should tell you," Princess grumbled irritably, darting furious glances at Dooley.

"We would be most grateful," I said. "Not to mention that if we find out who did this to Burt, our human—who, as I explained, works with the police—would help clear your human from any suspicion."

Princess frowned, working this over in her mind. "Okay, yeah, I'll bite," she said finally. "Last time I saw Shadow she was running for that door over there. This was moments after the explosion. She came shooting out of Philippe Goldsmith's room, Burt's grandson."

I glanced at the door Princess indicated. It was the same door Dooley and I had entered through. The fire escape. Like the cats at Vena's had speculated, Princess must have been spooked by the explosion and fled in a panic. She literally could be anywhere right now.

"Thank you so much," I said. "You've been a great help, Princess."

"Don't mention it," she said gruffly.

"You have a pee-pee, though, right?" asked Dooley, still mulling things over.

"Are you insane?!" yelled Princess. "Or just plain stoopid?!"

"I think it's time we moved on," I told Dooley, giving him a nudge.

"I'm just curious," said Dooley. "I never met a male female before. Or a female male."

"Get out of my face, dumbbell!" Princess bellowed. "I'm done talking to you haters!"

"Thank you, sir," said Dooley automatically as he turned to walk away.

The stream of vituperative language that followed was not something I'm prepared to repeat. Suffice it to say there were some very colorful statements made, and I picked up quite a few words I'd never heard before. Judging from Dooley's ears turning red and his face screwing up in surprise, he hadn't heard them before either. Then again, that's not saying much.

Just then, the doors to the elevator opened and Chase and Odelia stepped out.

CHAPTER 14

"So why did you want to meet here?" asked Odelia as Chase greeted her in the lobby of the Hampton Cove Star.

"I know how eager you must be to start interviewing suspects and tracking down leads, Poole, so I thought we might pool our resources."

"Poole—pool. I see what you did there."

He grinned. "I thought it was clever."

"But I thought you hadn't decided whether this was an accident or not?"

He sobered. "The fire marshals are still working on their report, but their preliminary findings suggest a highly explosive substance was used that could not have been present in the room under normal circumstances." He paused for effect. "Nitroglycerin features high on their list of suspected explosives."

She frowned. "Nitroglycerin? Do people still use that stuff?"

"It's still used in the mining, quarrying, demolition and construction industries. It's the active explosive in dynamite.

Used for drilling highway and railroad tunnels. Things like that. There's also an important medical application for the stuff, apparently. To treat certain heart conditions like angina pectoris and chronic heart failure."

"You've been reading up on your Wikipedia."

"Mostly what the fire marshal in charge told me. At any rate, at this point they're seriously looking into that bottle of beer that was brought in—figuring it probably contained something a lot more flammable and explosive than common household beer."

"An explosive beer bottle. Now that's something Burt would have appreciated. A most fascinating way to end his life."

"And it was sent up by a very compelling man."

"Curt Pigott. Didn't your people talk to him already?"

"Just routine questions. Your uncle Alec suggested we grill him a little more thoroughly." They'd approached the elevator and stood waiting for the cab to travel down. "How are your cats, by the way?"

She was touched by his concern. "They'll be fine. Thanks for telling me about the fleas."

He shrugged. "The least I can do. I care about the little darlings myself, you know."

It was the first time Chase had shown any interest what-soever in her cats, and she was pleasantly surprised. "I didn't know you were a cat person."

"Oh, sure. I've loved those funny furballs all my life. In fact I had a cat when I was a kid and I loved the little tyke to pieces. Was devastated when it died. Held it in my arms and wouldn't let it go until my mom told me Blackie was in heaven now, looking down upon me and following my further exploits with keen interest." He wiped at his eyes with his sleeve.

"Blackie?"

"He was a black cat."

"Right."

"They do tug at your heart, don't they?"

She watched with fascination as a tear rolled down his cheek. It was a side of him she hadn't seen before. A tenderness he hadn't displayed in her presence. It melted her heart.

They rode the elevator up in silence, as she wondered whether to tell him that she could actually communicate with her own little 'furballs.' Maybe at some point she would.

The elevator doors opened and to her surprise she saw that Max and Dooley were prancing along the corridor. "Hey, babes," she said. "What are you guys doing here?"

Chase laughed. "Funny. The way you speak cat."

Caught, she emitted a careless laugh. "Just, you know, saying hi."

Chase produced a few cat sounds himself. They were gibberish, of course, but it endeared him to her further. He crouched down next to Max and Dooley and tickled their tummies. "Hey, buddies," he said. "Fancy meeting you here. Are you lost? Are you poor babies lost? Don't worry. Your friend Chase is here. He'll take good care of you. Oh, yes, he will. Oh, yes, he will." At this, he picked up both cats and tucked them into his massive arms.

Max and Dooley, not used to this treatment, stared at Odelia in alarm. She signaled that it was fine and just to go with it. This new, cat-friendly Chase was a true revelation.

"Let's take them into the interview with us," she suggested.

"Won't they be a nui—I mean won't they be bored?" he asked.

"I'm sure they'll be on their best behavior," she said, giving her cats a wink.

Knocking on the door to the Most Compelling Man's room, Chase took a firmer grip on the cats, with Max and

Dooley still looking stunned by this unexpected development.

"Um, Odelia?" asked Max.

She glanced over.

"Why is your boyfriend pawing us like this?"

She merely smiled. Maybe one day she'd tell Chase about her secret, but today wasn't that day. She could tell him that some cats hate to be manhandled or picked up, though, but before she could, the door opened and a swarthy man dressed in a dressing gown appeared. His hair was pitch-black and gelled back, his face was the color of a mochaccino, and a smattering of dark chest hair came peeping from the top of his burgundy silk gown. He also looked slightly peeved. "Do you realize I ordered room service over half an hour ago? Standards at this hotel have seriously deteriorated since my last visit." He glanced at the cats Chase was holding. "Cats? I order bourbon and you bring me cats? Are you nuts?"

"We're not from the hotel, Mr. Pigott," Odelia said.

"Detective Chase Kingsley," said Chase, dislodging Max and thrusting out a hand. "Hampton Cove Police. And this is Odelia Poole. Civilian consultant with the department. We're here to ask you a couple of questions in regards to the murder of Burt Goldsmith."

The man's eyes went wide in consternation. "Murder? Police? Omigod!"

"May we step inside, sir? Easier to talk in the room than out here in the corridor."

"Oh, yes, of course," said the stricken actor. "Please come in, police people." He led the way into the nicely decorated room, if you disregarded the items of clothing strewn about everywhere and covering every available surface. Judging from the quality of the garments the man was a fastidious dresser. Perhaps even a most compelling one.

"Don't mind the mess," he said, waving a distracted hand and tugging his dressing gown closer around his trim physique. "I was just trying to decide what to wear for our get-together." When they stared at him, uncomprehending, he grimaced. "As you probably know, we're holding a thing in town. The Seabreeze Music Center graciously accepted to host us for a three-day conference on all things interesting, fascinating, compelling, intriguing and I'm probably forget-ting a few adjectives. But with this darned Burt-getting-blown-up thing we're seriously considering calling the whole thing off. It really would be in awfully bad taste."

Chase, still holding on to the cats, who were squirming in his grip, said, "I understand you sent a bottle of Dos Siglas up to Burt Goldsmith's room just before he died?"

The man's dark eyebrows wiggled. "No, sir, I did not. I never sent anything to Burt's room. Oh, I know he kept accusing me of doing so—taunting him, as he called it. But I assured both him and your colleagues who were in here badgering me before that whoever sent those bottles, it wasn't me. I disliked Burt intensely and the feeling was mutual. If I could avoid having anything to do with the man I did. The fact that we were in Hampton Cove together—at the same hotel, no less—was cause for serious discomfort on my part."

"You didn't choose this time and place to coincide with Burt's shoot?" asked Odelia.

"No, I did not. None of us did. It was the other way around. We put on this conference and then Burt decided to drop by unannounced, no doubt trying to steal our thunder. The conference has attracted a lot of attention and Burt, who was a real attention whore if you pardon my French, couldn't resist the temptation to bask in our limelight."

A black cat had entered the room from the balcony and

stood perfectly still, eyeing Max and Dooley with menace. Uh-oh.

"So you never sent up that bottle?" asked Chase, struggling to contain Odelia's cats.

"No, detective, I didn't," said the Most Compelling Man in the World haughtily. "This hotel doesn't even carry Tres Siglas, which goes to show how low standards have dropped. Furthermore, I don't understand the significance of this bottle. Who cares what beer Burt drank? It certainly wasn't Tres Siglas. It wasn't even Dos Siglas, the brand he represented. Burt hated beer. Said it tasted like dishwater. He preferred his liquor strong and undiluted."

Chase finally gave up the battle and dropped Max and Dooley to the floor. They stood poised, watching Curt's cat intently, every muscle in their small bodies flexed.

"It would appear that the final bottle you sent up—or someone else sent up—contained the powerful explosive that ended Burt Goldsmith's life," said Chase. "Which is why it's imperative we find out who sent that bottle."

The man's jaw dropped. "An exploding bottle of beer? Oh, my. Oh, dear me." Suddenly his face twisted into an expression of peevishness. He stomped his foot. "That foul old bird! Can't you see what's going on here, detective? Can't you read between the lines? He sent it to himself! Burt sent that bottle to himself! He wanted to go out with a bang and he did! Now every newspaper in the country will headline the story— people will be talking about this for days. He wanted to best us one final time. Oh, the horrible, nasty old bird!"

"You think he killed himself?" asked Odelia, surprised.

Curt Pigott swung his arms. "Of course he did! The man was pushing eighty. He didn't have a lot of time left. And it wouldn't surprise me if he wasn't sick from some wasting disease, judging from the way he'd lost the pounds in recent years. He wanted to kick the bucket on his own terms and put in one last performance. A most fascinating death."

It was a most interesting theory—one Chase seemed to consider credible, judging from the way he was rubbing his chin. "Room service staff said the order to bring up those bottles came from your room," he said.

"I swear to you, detective—I had nothing to do with it! And how easy would it be to tell room service that I gave the commission. There are no papers to sign when you call down an order—simply a phone call and the mention of your room number. Anyone could have given my name and number—anyone at all." He wagged a finger in their faces, his own face clouding. "Especially Burt Goldsmith, who was a cunning old coot right up until the very end. He knew he could get me into hot water with this stunt. One final blow. One final insult."

"I take it the dislike between you two was mutual?" asked Odelia.

"Oh, it most assuredly was." He tapped his hairy chest. "*I* was supposed to be the Most Fascinating Man in the World. *Me!* Dos Siglas asked me first. But Burt, who was a down-on-his-luck two-bit actor at the time, decided to improve his chances by sleeping with the casting lady. The rest is history. Fifteen years later he's the star and I'm the also-ran. And ever since he's been rubbing it in my face," he added between gritted teeth.

The guy definitely had motive, Odelia decided. He seemed to hate Burt's guts with a vengeance. But did he do it? Hard to prove. Unless they found trace evidence of the nitroglycerin on his person or this hotel room, they didn't have a lot to go on.

Just then, war broke out in the room. The black cat, who'd been staring down Max and Dooley, suddenly jumped their bones, and for the next few minutes the world was a maelstrom of claws, piercing yowls and screams, and fur flying all over the place.

The fight began in the center of the room, then moved across its full acreage.

"Max! Dooley!" Odelia cried, desperately trying to separate the warring parties.

It's hard to stop a cat fight, though. Cats tend to get caught up in the melee, and lash out indifferent of whether the other party is friend or foe. In other words, you step in at your own peril.

And as the fight moved towards the bed, suddenly Chase stepped to the fore, picked up two cats in his right hand, another in his left hand, and pulled. There was a rending sound, and when finally the smoke and fur cleared, he had effectively broken up the fight.

Odelia stared at the man, and so did Curt Pigott.

"You, sir, are marvelous!" Curt exclaimed, and Odelia couldn't have put it better.

CHAPTER 15

$\mathcal{I}$ was feeling slightly dazed. Being in a huge fight with a princess will do that to a cat. Princess might be slightly clueless about whether he or she was a she or a he but they definitely fought like a tomcat and I had the scratches and the bite marks to prove it. I was tucked away in the crook of Chase's right arm while Dooley was tucked away in the crook of the burly cop's left arm. All in all it was a decent proposition and I was slowly starting to feel safe again. To serve and protect was one of those mottos I'd never given much thought, but now that I saw that it extended to me, myself and mine, I was all on board. I was a fan.

"That was a wonderful thing you did back there, Chase," said Odelia as we descended down to the lobby in the hotel elevator.

"Just doing my job," Chase grunted, though I could sense Odelia's words pleased him.

"No, I mean, you could have gotten yourself hurt. That cat meant business."

"Eh. Just a little pussycat. What harm can it do?"

"Did you see those claws?" Dooley cried. "That cat was going for the kill."

Muzak softly played on the elevator sound system. 'Raindrops are falling on my head,' someone crooned. A cat had just fallen on my head, and Chase had saved us. Suddenly I was feeling all warm and fuzzy, and gave the cop's square chin a nudge with the top of my head.

"Aww," Odelia said.

"Hrmph," Chase said, stiffening.

I could be mistaken, but I had the distinct impression Chase was not a cat person, and he was merely doing this to get in good with Odelia. I would have said he did it to get in bed with Odelia, but he'd already accomplished that particular feat. So what was he after?

"Babies!" Dooley cried suddenly.

I turned to him. "What are you talking about, Dooley?"

"He wants babies! That's why he's being so nice to us all of a sudden!"

I hate to admit it but once in a while Dooley gets it right. Now was such an occasion. There's only one reason why a dog person would suddenly turn into a cat person—or at least pretend to do so: the old baby maker is stirring its ugly head. "You know what, Dooley?" I said. "I think you just might be right." Then again, maybe a couple of babies wasn't so bad?

'Because I'm free. Nothing's worrying me.'

The elevator dinged and the doors opened, allowing us a nice view of the lobby. I had no idea why Chase insisted on carrying us. We might have been dinged a little, and lost some of our fur and a lot of our dignity, but my paws still worked. And yet I didn't stir from my comfortable perch, and neither did Dooley. As far as I was concerned, Chase could make as many babies with Odelia as he liked. I'd suddenly grown quite fond of the sturdy cop. First he'd turned out to be Hampton Cove's fiercest fleaslayer, and now he'd saved our lives.

We walked through the lobby and past the hotel restaurant when a curious sight met our eyes. As one man—or one woman—or one cat—our small company halted in its tracks.

Chase frowned. "Isn't that—"

"Grandma!" Odelia cried. "She's at it again."

I don't know what she was referring to. Grandma Muffin was having lunch with a bespectacled young man who reminded me of John-Boy of *The Waltons* fame. He was pale and self-conscious and kept laughing at Grandma's dubious jokes. The old lady, meanwhile—Dooley's human, coincidentally—was dressed up like—there's no other word for it—a tart. She was sporting the kind of cleavage usually reserved for women with more assets than the bony old woman possessed, and the whole thing fell kind of flat. Her face was painted with various types of makeup, and she had on the sort of hat that other, more extravagant and loud women could get away with. Not her. Nor could she get away with the lime-colored fluorescent dress she was wearing. Queen of England Grandma Muffin is not.

Before I had hitched up my lower mandible, Odelia was already stalking in the direction of her grandmother. Chase reluctantly followed in her wake.

"Gran, what are you doing here?" Odelia demanded with not a little heat.

Grandma looked up with a supercilious glint in her eye. She might not be the Queen of England but she could do a fine impression of condescending snootiness. "And who might you be, young lady?" she asked.

"Gran! What on earth has gotten into you?"

Grandma turned to her lunch date. "I'm sorry about this. She must be mistaking me for someone else." Then she leaned into Odelia and hissed, "Beat it, missy. Can't you see I'm buttering up my grandson?"

The grandson in question didn't hide his discomfort. He went so far as to dart apologetic glances at Chase, who stood watching the scene with the kind of inscrutability and thousand-yard stare cops learn during their first week at police academy.

"You're coming home with me right now," Odelia snapped. "Get up. Now!"

"Get lost! Now!" Grandma retorted smartly. "You're cramping my style!"

"Oh, for God's sakes," Odelia said.

I could have pointed out that it wasn't God who'd put Grandma up to this, but I had a feeling keeping mum was the safer option at this juncture. Safe behind the bulwark of Chase Kingsley's brawny arms, Dooley and I had front-row seats to the show that was about to begin, and I for one was ready to enjoy it to its full potential. I'd never seen Odelia and her grandmother square off before, and it promised to be a corker.

Just then, a third party joined the fray. I recognized her as Scarlett Canyon, and she had the dizzyingly deep neckline to live up to her last name.

"Ooh, Philippe, darling. I thought I'd find you here," she purred as she swooped down on the pale youth, and smothered him with both kisses and some prime real estate.

"Get off him, you tramp!" Gran snapped, indignant. "That's my grandson you're slobbering over!"

Scarlett straightened, allowing Philippe to come up for air and adjust his glasses. "Did you say something, you bony old witch?"

"I said that's my grandson! Get away from him!"

Scarlett wrapped her arms possessively around the young man, draping herself all over him in the process. Once again his glasses—steamed up by now—went askew. "He's mine, Vesta. All mine. I mothered his father and I won't let you take him away from me again."

"I mothered his father!"

"Says you."

"I think I would remember giving birth to a fine specimen like… Burt Goldsmith's son."

Scarlett threw her head back in a raucous laugh. "You don't even know his name, do you?"

"I do," said Gran, a dark frown marring her features. "His name is…" She darted a hopeful look at Philippe, trying to cast him in the role of her personal prompter. But Philippe Goldsmith was struggling with the weight of Scarlett's full-bodied presence on his shoulders and was momentarily lost to the world.

"His name was Hunter Goldsmith. I say 'was' because he died—from a broken heart because he missed his dear precious mother so. And why do I know these things? Because I christened him Hunter before Burt and I were so brutally separated by his unfeeling and cold-hearted parents." Scarlett sniffed theatrically. "Which is why his death comes as such a shocking blow. Our final chance at the happy reunion. Ripped away by cruel, cruel fate!"

"Oh, you're full of crap," Grandma said, and made a menacing step in her rival's direction. "I'll show you what cruel, cruel fate can do to a painted hussy like you!"

Scarlett reared back, but before Gran could act out her threat, Chase stepped between the two women. I don't know how he did it, for he had his arms full of feline, but he still managed to act the perfect traffic cop, holding up his hands at the two old ladies.

"You're coming with us now," he growled at Grandma, who nodded reluctantly. And to Scarlett, he grunted, "And you better behave, Mrs. Canyon, or I'll have to write you up for disorderly conduct, you understand?"

The woman knew better than to protest, and nodded furiously. But when Gran's back was turned, she still managed to stick out her tongue at her longtime nemesis.

"I'm starting to like this Chase guy, Max," said Dooley. "First he breaks up a vicious cat fight and now a nasty old lady fight. I don't know how he does it but he does it very well."

"The man is a god amongst men," I agreed.

And then we were finally on our way home. Not a moment too soon. I enjoy helping out my human, but the awful truth of the matter is: sometimes it's hard to be a cat.

CHAPTER 16

The Pooles were all gathered in Tex and Marge's kitchen: Odelia, Marge and Alec standing in a small circle around Gran, who was seated at the kitchen table, like a suspect at the police station, or an accused standing trial. Chase had left, wisely deciding this was a matter best handled by the family and not wanting to interfere. Tex, meanwhile, was busying himself washing the dishes, though judging from the clatter of cups and plates smashing against each other he was more engaged in blowing off some much-needed steam.

"I'm telling you nicely, Ma," said Uncle Alec. "Drop this nonsense right this minute."

"I'm not dropping this nonsense," said Gran stubbornly. "Philippe Goldsmith is a nice young man and he is my grandson. Can I help it if he's taken such a shine to me? He says he'll put me up in the Goldsmith mansion someplace in Colorado and pamper me for the rest of my natural life." She held up her wrinkly hands. "It's an offer I can't possibly refuse!"

"It's an offer you will refuse," said Marge. "Because you're

96

not Philippe's grandmother. There's no way you had a child and then promptly forgot about it."

"Yes, you may be daft but you're not that daft," grumbled Alec.

"Watch your tongue," Gran warned. "I am still your mother."

"Yes, you are. *My* mother—not this Hunter Goldsmith, whoever he was."

"Nice name, Hunter," mused Grandma. "I can't remember giving it to him but I must have. Just the kind of name I would have given a healthy baby boy." She darted a quick look at Alec. "Your dad named you, of course. I wanted to call you Filip and Marge Sandra."

Alec and Marge glanced at one another. "F. Lip and S. Lip. Flip and Slip. Nice one, Ma," Alec said. "Good thing you left the naming to Dad."

Grandma shrugged. "They're nice-sounding names. Not like Alec and Marge. I've always hated those names."

"And you're telling us now," said Marge.

"I'm sorry, dear," said Grandma. "You had to find out sometime. Why not now, when I'm moving on to my first family?" She patted Mom's cheek. "I like this family, I really do, but I was born to be a woman of substance, and my ship has finally come in."

Dad made a disgusted sound and chipped some more China. Odelia decided this was ridiculous. "You can't really expect the Goldsmiths to take your word for this, Gran," she said. "They're bound to do a DNA test—see if you're really related or some kind of con artist."

"Oh, they already did," said Gran in a careless tone. "Philippe is a very meticulous young man—he had his personal physician take a swab of my saliva and said the lab will fast-track the processing. Until then I'm a guest at his home. His casa is my casa. Those were his exact words." She smiled beatifically. "Such a nice young man. Intelligent, rich, well-spoken. I'm glad my absence from his life hasn't held him back. Of course now that we found each other I'll be a major influence on him. He'll finally flourish and reach his full potential."

Tex squeezed some more unintelligible noises from his throat.

"He might even name a school after me," Gran continued. "The Goldsmiths are big on education. Major contributors to the University of Colorado and other local institutions of higher education. I'll fit right in. I'm big on education myself."

"You dropped out of school when you were sixteen!" Alec cried.

"And I've regretted it since," she insisted. She smiled. "Maybe I'll go back to school. Get a degree in astrophysics or something. I could work for NASA. The sky is the limit now."

"Gran, this is crazy," said Odelia. "The test results will show that you're not related and the Goldsmiths will ship you right back home!"

"No, they won't," said the old lady stubbornly. "First of all I did have Burt's child—even if my memory is a little fuzzy on the details. And secondly I intend to ingratiate myself to the Goldsmiths in such a way that they'll consider me their honorary grandmother." She nodded decidedly. "One way or another, I'm a Goldsmith now, and I fully intend to live up to the name. I might even run for governor of Colorado. Isn't that what rich people do? But first I need to get my NASA degree. Tom Hanks is waiting for me up there in Apollo 13."

"Please, God, take me now," muttered Dad, and threw down the dish brush.

CHAPTER 17

I stared at Brutus who was staring at the box of pills Odelia had bought. The box of pills were Vena's idea. After examining the brutish black cat—though a lot less brutish since he'd confided his big secret in me—she'd determined everything was A-Okay with his plumbing. Which told her the issue was between his ears. No idea what she meant by that. Vena also said he needed a shrink, but since cat shrinks are hard to find she decided to give him some pills to alleviate his predicament. It should put the pep right back in his pee-pee.

Before leaving the house, Odelia laid out a couple of pills, and told Brutus to take one with a little water. And now Brutus was staring at the pills and I was staring at him. And since Dooley was staring at me staring at Brutus staring at the pills, things were a little awkward.

Harriet, of course, was staring at herself. In the mirror in the bathroom. She'd discovered that if she jumped on top of the wash basin, she could study herself to her heart's content, which was what she was doing right now.

"I don't like it, Max," Dooley said finally.

"What don't you like, Dooley?" I said.

"The collar. Makes you look weird."

Just what I needed. A motivational speech.

"That's because collars look weird on all cats, Dooley," I pointed out. "Because cats weren't designed to wear collars."

"I know that. But on you it looks extra weird. Probably because it's too tight. I can see all kinds of flab sticking out. Like someone tied a rubber band around a whale."

He was right. Vena had used the final hole punched into the collar and still it was too tight around my neck. I'd told Odelia it was because the collar was too small. Vena had said it was because I was too fat, and she'd threatened to put me on another one of her diets. In her infinite wisdom Odelia had decided that the diet would have to wait until after the flea ordeal had been dealt with. I hoped by then she would have forgotten about the diet thing.

"Just take it already," I told Brutus, tiring of this waiting game.

He chewed his lower lip. "I don't know, Max. What if my pee-pee falls off?"

"Why would your pee-pee fall off?"

"I read about these pills. There's always side effects. And one of the side effects is that your pee-pee swells up and dies. What am I going to tell Harriet if my pee-pee dies?"

"Your pee-pee isn't going to die from a teeny tiny pill. Just think how happy Harriet will be if your machinery works like it should. Focus on the light, Brutus, not the darkness."

Dooley transferred his attention from my tight collar to Brutus. "What's his deal?" he asked. Then he remembered. "Oh, the pee-pee thing. Right."

Brutus's eyes went wide. "You told him?!"

"Of course I told him. He's my best friend."

"I told you in confidence!"

"And I told Dooley in confidence."

He groaned. "Tell me you didn't tell Harriet."

"I didn't tell Harriet," said Dooley. "So why don't you take the pill, Brutus?"

His bedside manners were a little lacking in tact and delicacy, I felt, and some of the old rancor had slipped back into his tone. It was obvious my helping Brutus still rankled.

"Are you deaf? I just told Max about the side effects."

"So what if your thingy falls off? Who cares?"

"I care! And Harriet will care if I can't…" He chewed his lip again.

"She'll find another boyfriend," said Dooley carelessly. "Plenty of cats in the sea."

Brutus gave him a look that could kill, and I had the distinct impression another cat fight was brewing. And since Chase wasn't here to break up the fight, I told Dooley, "Go look for Odelia's pill, Dooley. I'm sure it's in the bathroom upstairs somewhere."

His eyes lit up, like I knew they would. "She has the pill?"

"She has the pill. I'm one hundred percent sure." More like fifty percent, but giving false hope is one of the secrets of making friends and influencing cats.

And off he was, at a happy trot. If he could find proof that Odelia was on the pill, and not about to pop out a litter of babies, he would finally be happy. And Brutus and I would have some peace and quiet to think this other pill thing through.

"Just take it," I told Brutus. "See what happens."

"Why don't you take it? Then if your pee-pee stays firmly attached I'll know it's safe."

I laughed. "I don't have issues, Brutus. You do."

"Don't remind me," he grunted, and unsheathed a sharp claw.

I gulped. Brutus might be domesticated, to some extent, but there was still something of the wild animal in him.

"Okay, fine," I said. "I'll take one if you'll take one. How is that?"

He sheathed the claw. "You would do that for me?"

"Of course."

"Oh, Max—you're a real pal," he said, visibly touched.

As long as he stopped whining about his pee-pee, I was prepared to take any pill.

So I jumped on top of the chair, then on top of the table, and gobbled up one of the pills Odelia had laid out. I didn't even need to take it with a little water. Brutus, who'd made the jump to the table in one go—admittedly he is a little slimmer than me—swallowed his pill. And then we stared at one another. Slowly, but inexorably, our gazes lowered. Then, realizing what we were doing, we both looked away again.

"I don't feel nothing," said Brutus after a moment.

"I don't feel nothing either," I confessed.

"Let's take another pill," said Brutus.

"I'm not taking another pill," I said.

"Chicken."

"Not!"

"Then take it."

"You take it."

"Oh, I will," he said, and gobbled up another pill, crunching it between his teeth.

I couldn't say no. My whole cathood depended on it. So I followed suit.

More minutes passed. Nothing happened.

"Maybe we should take another one," said Brutus.

I decided this time to beat him to it, and we both dove for the pills.

Just as I was gobbling down pill number five, feeling mighty manly, Dooley strode in, looking a little pale around the nostrils.

"You guys," he said, retching slightly. "I don't feel so good."

"What happened?" I asked.

"I found Odelia's pills."

"Hey, that's good, right?"

"And then I ate one."

"You did what?"

He retched some more. "They looked like white kibble!"

"Oh, Dooley," I said, and then I retched, too.

Truth be told, I wasn't feeling so hot myself.

And when I glanced over at Brutus, he looked like he was about to pass out.

Five minutes later, when Odelia walked in, back from giving Grandma the tongue-lashing the old lady deserved, she found three cats puking their guts out, with a fourth, Harriet, wearily shaking her head at so much tomfoolery. Then Harriet dug her teeth into her collar for some reason and moments later joined the rest of us in the puking department.

CHAPTER 18

As Odelia walked out of the house, laden with cats, she bumped into Chase, who immediately offered to take over some of the furry creatures. She unloaded Brutus and Harriet in his arms and took Max and Dooley into the car, followed by the new cat lover.

"What's wrong with them?" he asked as he placed Brutus and Harriet on the backseat.

She took a deep breath. "As far as I can tell," she said, slipping behind the wheel as Chase dropped down in the passenger seat, "Brutus ate too many vitamin tablets, so did Max, Dooley ate one of my pills, and Harriet tried to chew through her collar."

"It doesn't look good on me," the white cat said, panting heavily. "Cramps my style."

Chase directed a worried look at the foursome in the backseat. "You think they'll live?"

"We're gonna die!" Dooley cried. "I knew it! We're dead meat!"

"They'll live," Odelia said, stomping on the accelerator.

The car jumped away from the curb and then they were on their way to Vena—for the second time that day.

"Thank God," said Chase. "I love the little suckers to death. Especially Max. He's such a special cat, don't you think? I don't think I've ever felt like that about any animal. Truth."

She frowned. He was laying it on a little thick now. "Max is great," she said curtly. When he wasn't getting into a pill-swallowing competition with Brutus.

"Oh, he's fantastic," said Chase, slapping his thigh. "I love the little guy to death. Never thought I could ever love a cat again, I mean—after what happened to Smokey."

"I thought your cat's name was Blackie?"

"That's what I meant. Blackie. Dear, sweet Blackie."

She cut a quick glance sideways. Damn, the man looked good in profile. "Did you and Uncle Alec happen to talk about Max, by any chance?"

"Nope," he said, feigning innocence. "Not a word. Me and Alec? We talk about the Yankees and the Mets, about work, and that's it. Not a word about cats. Why would we?"

She had the distinct impression that this sudden fondness of cats didn't come out of nowhere. Alec had probably told Chase that the surest way to his niece's heart was through her cats. Why else would he be all over Max all of a sudden? "You know? Now that you and Max have developed such a strong and powerful bond, maybe you can do me a favor?"

"Sure. Anything. Anything for sweet, sweet Maxie."

"Ugh," Max groaned from the backseat, then retched some more.

"With Grandma giving us all such a hard time, I feel I should spend some time at my parents' house. Try to talk some sense into the old lady. Can I rely on you to catsit for me?"

He seemed taken aback. "Catsit?"

"Yeah, just, you know, make sure they're fed and cleaned —Vena gave me a flea comb to apply with a little bit of soapy water—and don't forget to clean out their litter box."

He made a face. "Litter box?"

"You know, remove the old litter, scrape out the clumps of pee stuck to the bottom, wash it out with soapy water—I like to add a little bleach, too. For some reason Max loves the scent of bleach, don't ask me why. Take a fresh sponge and a fresh pair of gloves—I hope they're not too small for you. It's one size fits all, though, so you should be good. Towel the box dry—use paper towels, not kitchen towels—and fill it up with about three to five inches of litter and you're done." She shrugged. "I don't know why I'm telling you, though, seeing as you're an even bigger cat person than I am. You've probably done this a million times."

For a moment, Chase didn't speak, then he said, a catch in his voice, "I may not be a bigger cat person than you, though, babe."

"Oh?"

"The thing is—Alec told me to be extra-nice to your cats."

"Now why would he say a thing like that?"

He turned to her. "The thing is, I like you, Odelia. I like you a lot. In fact it's not too much to say I like you a whole damn lot—probably more than I've liked any woman."

Her face flushed, as she realized four cats were holding their breaths in the backseat.

"I like spending time with you. I like coming home to you. I like sleeping with you. Heck, I've never felt happier than these past few months we've spent together." He took a deep breath. "I like your cats, but I like you a lot more. I know you're a package deal, babe. One woman and a litter of crazy cats. And that's fine. In fact it's more than fine. What I'm trying to say is…" He lowered his voice. "How do you feel about moving in together?"

She smiled and darted a quick look in the rearview mirror at her menagerie. They were still holding their breaths, or so it seemed. "Breathe, you guys," she said. "Deep breaths." She applied the same advice to herself, then looked over at Chase and spoke a single word. "Yes."

Chase pumped the air with his fist. "One catsitter, free of charge, at your service."

She laughed. "You don't have to catsit. I was just joshing you."

"Oh, thank God," he said, throwing his head back.

"I thought you were so busted up when Blackie died? Or was it Smokey?"

"I was busted up when Blackie *and* Smokey died. Both of them. I had Blackie when I was six. And my folks got me Smokey when I was twelve. Those two were with me for many wonderful years. Only Smokey was a Lab and Blackie was a Golden Retriever. Best dogs a man has ever known. I still miss 'em every day."

"Oh, I'm so sorry, Chase. Maybe we should get a dog?"

There was a collective intake of breath behind Odelia.

"Four cats and a dog? Don't you think that's a bit much?"

She patted his leg. "We'll figure it out."

Can a cat person peacefully coexist with a dog person? She had no idea, but she was willing to try.

"A dog," Harriet said, a whining note in her voice. "She's getting a dog. I hate dogs."

"He's moving in," said Dooley, sounding shell-shocked. "He'll eat all her pills and then there will be babies!"

"Oh, relax, you guys," said Max. "Chase is okay. He saved us from that wild cat."

"That's true," said Dooley musingly. "There may be hope for us yet."

"My pee-pee," said Brutus suddenly, interrupting the others. "It hurts."

"Jeezus, Brutus," said Max. "What is that thing?"

"Is that…" Harriet began, then cried, "Brutus, it's huge!"

"And painful!" he cried. "Owowowow!"

"Didn't you take the same pills, Max?" asked Dooley.

"I did."

"Yours is tiny," Harriet said with distaste. "Miniscule. Almost non-existent."

Max sighed, the sigh of a long-suffering cat. "Why me?" he said.

"Are they all right?" asked Chase, turning in his seat to look back.

"They're fine," she assured him. At least she hoped they were.

CHAPTER 19

hat night, we were all sufficiently recovered to attend cat choir, which is just about the biggest social event for cats in Hampton Cove. Cat choir is all about letting our inner cat out and sing to its heart's content. The only drawback is that the neighbors of Hampton Cove Park are cultural barbarians who don't appreciate the finer points of cat-produced art.

We don't care, though, and carry on regardless of the catcalls and shoes thrown.

That night the meeting was a sad affair, though. All members were wearing their flea collars—perhaps the rest of the world had abandoned the terrible practice of outfitting cats with collars when the first flea reared its ugly head, but here in Hampton Cove the collar still reigned supreme, or so it seemed. There's nothing to put a good cat down like the collar does, and we were all suffering the indignation. Even Shanille, our conductor, was downcast.

Brutus, recovered from his vitamin poisoning, for that was what he had apparently suffered, Dooley, the consumption of Odelia's pill having had as its worst effect a slight case

of diarrhea, and Harriet, vowing never to ingest flea-repel-
lent ever again, were all present and accounted for. On me,
those vitamin pills Vena had prescribed for Brutus merely
had the effect of boosting my energy levels to such an extent
that I was feeling fit as a fiddle.

So when suddenly Princess, the Most Compelling Cat in
the World, showed up, along with a troupe of other cats I'd
never seen, I felt oddly complacent. In fact I would have told
the black cat to 'bring it on!' had it not been for my innate
sense of self-preservation. Also, that scratch across the left
butt cheek still hurt, and I wasn't looking to turn the other
cheek.

"Who are those cats?" asked Harriet as she stared in abject
fascination.

And I had to admit that the small troupe of cats looked
absolutely amazing.

For one thing, none of them were wearing flea collars,
which made them stand out. And for another, they entered
the scene with a marked swagger, as if they owned the place.
You cannot own a park, of course, but it was obvious nobody
had told them.

"Isn't that..." Dooley said, his voice dying away. "Max, it's
Princess!"

Princess raised her paw. "We come in peace!" she
declared, loud enough for the entire gathering to hear. "And
we come bearing gifts!" she added, gesturing to her friends.

One by one, the cats stepped to the fore, tapping their
chests and introducing themselves. "My name is Princess,"
said Princess. "The Most Compelling Cat in the World."

"My name is Beca, and I'm the Most Attractive Cat in the
World," a fit red cat said.

"I'm Chloe," said a pretty striped cat. "And I'm the Most
Intriguing Cat in the World."

"I'm Aubrey and I'm the Most Iconic Cat in the World," said a strapping white cat.

"And I'm Fat Amy, and I'm the Sexiest Cat Alive," a well-rounded cat said.

"And together we're the Most Interesting Cats in the World!" Princess yelled.

And suddenly, before our very eyes, the cats started performing the kind of routine one habitually sees on the stage of some Broadway musical. Or in those funny *Pitch Perfect* movies. They launched into a song-and-dance routine that had us all staring in abject awe.

They started off with a bit of Taylor Swift's *Shake it Off*, shaking their tails provocatively, flawlessly segued into Beyoncé's *Crazy in Love*, synchronized dancing to the beat, then it was on to Gwen Stefani's *Hollaback Girl* before finishing off with a rousing rendition of Pink's *Get The Party Started*, really blowing up the scene, dancing up a storm.

When the show was over, we all blew out a collective gasp of appreciation, then the entire cat choir burst into a loud and raucous applause.

The interesting cat collective stood panting for a moment, basking in the admiration, then took a slight bow, with Princess declaring, "Now it's time for you guys to blow *us* away!"

I gulped, and so did some of the other members of cat choir. Truth be told, our repertoire is a little limited. Cat choir isn't so much about putting on a compelling show but more about giving local cats a chance to shoot the breeze and sniff each other's butts. And that's what some of the members now did, approaching the Most Interesting Cats in the World and sniffing their butts. I could have told them this was not a good idea, but some cats can't be told and need to be shown. A few harsh words and well-aimed lashes of razor-sharp claws later, five cats were racing away into the tree line with their tails between their legs.

"Let's do what we do best, fellas," said Kingman. "Let's sing our anthem!"

We all gave him a bewildered look. Anthem? Did we have an anthem?

But Shanille seemed to have picked up on his cue, for she cried over the hubbub that followed Kingman's words, "From the top—one and two and three and four!" And proceeded to belt out, "*Midnight. Not a sound from the pavement. Has the moon lost her—*"

"Has she lost her mind?" asked Harriet next to me. "I can't sing that."

Shanille was doing little movements with her paws, dancing in a circle, head and tail held high, just the way they did it in the musical *Cats*. I'd only seen it once. On YouTube. And it had failed to impress. Though I had to admit I enjoyed Barbra's version of the hit song.

Other cats soon fell in, caterwauling with absolute abandon, the yowls and ear-splitting screeches lighting up windows all along the streets that lined the park. Soon voices could be heard from neighbors, and next thing we knew the shoes were raining down.

As Dooley dodged one particularly well-aimed shoe, he said, "Don't these people ever run out of footwear?"

Apparently not. Meanwhile, Shanille was undeterred, and kept giving her moving rendition of *Memory*, swaying to the music like a cat under the influence of a powerful narcotic, possibly marijuana or some other hallucinatory substance. Other cats mimicked her movements, turning the performance into something akin to a first-grade school play.

The Most Interesting Cats in the World where mostly unimpressed. Shaking their heads, they decided not to stick around and left the scene before the grand finale, chuckling at the sad show. Looked like the visitors had won this particular competition.

Shanille hadn't even noticed her audience had dispersed, for she kept belting out those hard-to-reach high notes. The moment her final shriek died away, she took a bow and a size-fifteen combat boot in the small of her back and was out for the count.

Things kind of petered out after that. The neighbor who'd thrown the boot must have known that if you want to defeat an army you take out its leader. With Shanille down, there was no sense sticking around, and we decided to set a course for the good old homestead.

"Shanille did well," Dooley said. "She has a really good voice."

"I thought she sucked," Harriet commented, harsh theater critic that she was.

"But what about those Most Interesting Cats, huh?" said Brutus hoarsely. It was obvious those five cats had left an indelible impression on his impressionable soul.

Harriet snapped her head up. "If you like them so much, why don't you join them!"

And with this crack, she stalked off, tail in the air.

"Harriet!" he cried after her. "I didn't mean it like that!"

"Oh, yes, you did!"

"No, I didn't! Harriet—come back!"

We watched as Brutus trotted after his mate. And then it was just me and Dooley.

"You know, we still haven't found Burt's cat Shadow," he said.

"Yeah, we should probably have asked those other interesting cats." Dooley had reminded me that we were seriously remiss in our duty towards our human: we had a crime to solve, and all this gallivanting around had put a serious crimp in our sleuthing efforts.

"Max?"

"Mh?"

"If Grandma moves out, do you think she'll take me along with her to Colorado?"

I stared at my friend in shock. "You think so?"

He shrugged as we paused underneath a streetlamp. The hubbub of cat choir and its army of shoe-throwing fans were reduced to mere echoes, the soft sounds of the night now all around us. There was a nip in the air, and an owl was stoically hooting somewhere nearby.

"I don't want to move to Colorado, Max. I like my life in Hampton Cove. I have my friends here." He gestured at me. "And I have Odelia and Marge and Tex. I like Grandma, of course. She is my human. And if she moves away I guess I'll move away, too. But I don't mind telling you I don't like it." He shook his head sadly. "No, sir, I don't like it one bit."

"I don't like it either," I admitted. "I don't want you to move away, Dooley."

He heaved a deep sigh. "Well, let's hope she stays. Then I can stay, too."

We walked on. There was a soft rustling sound in the underbrush, and moments later a small rodent came peeping its twitchy nose out. It was a mouse. A nice, white, juicy mouse. The kind of mouse any able-bodied cat like me or Dooley would have enjoyed to chase.

It was a testament to our mood that we didn't even give it a second glance.

CHAPTER 20

*O*delia awoke in the middle of the night from a sense that something was amiss. It took her a few moments to realize what it was: no cats. Usually Max slept at the foot of the bed—at least when he wasn't out and about, exploring Hampton Cove with his friends. After the ordeal he'd had, that was probably what he was doing right now.

Since she was up, she decided to head down to the kitchen for a glass of milk.

Next to her, the figure of Chase stirred. The cop was sound asleep, his arm draped across his pillow, his tousled hair visible in the diffuse light of a moon curiously peeping through the curtains.

She smiled. Now wasn't that a sight for sore eyes? It was a long time since a man had slept in her bed, and this partic-ular man was something else indeed. As she slipped her feet into her slippers, she thought about his words. Move in together? Was she ready for that?

She padded across the hardwood floor to the door, careful not to make a sound, and then snuck downstairs. In the kitchen she poured some milk into her Fozzie Bear cup and placed it in the microwave, then leaned against the kitchen counter and crossed her arms. Through the kitchen window she could see the backyard, still plunged into darkness, the moon generously sprinkling its milky white light upon the world below.

The cat door hung motionless, and Max's bowls were untouched, a testament to his roaming ways. He was probably in the park, where he and others of his kind enjoyed spending part of their nights. Cats are nocturnal animals, and like to be out and about while the rest of the world sleeps. She just hoped he was all right, and so were the others.

And as the microwave softly dinged and she took the cup between her hands and attempted a first sip of the warm brew, she closed her eyes. When she opened them again, Chase was walking into the kitchen, yawning, and she smiled.

"Up already?" he asked, joining her.

"Couldn't sleep," she admitted, and held up her cup. "Want some?"

"Sure. I'll take mine with a little honey."

"The man has a sweet tooth."

"He sure has," he said with a wolfish grin, and pulled her close, planting a kiss on her lips. It wasn't the heat from the milk that spread through her but a completely different kind of heat. One she could definitely get used to. She didn't know if it would help her sleep but suddenly she didn't care so much about sleep anymore.

There was more kissing, and the cup of milk was soon transferred to the counter and so was her perky behind.

She wasn't sure if she wanted Chase to move in with her, but she sure as heck wanted him to keep kissing her like this and bending her backwards over the countertop.

When they both came up for air, he took a sip from her

cup and looked at her over the rim with those dark eyes of his. Something stirred and she said, "Let's go back to bed."

He smiled. "Thought you'd never ask."

By the time Max and Dooley strolled in, Odelia and Chase were fast asleep, enjoying a well-deserved rest after some very strenuous midnight activities.

CHAPTER 21

The next morning, Odelia joined Chase as they drove off to work. He'd scheduled four more interviews with four more very interesting men, and wanted her there. He claimed she had a knack for getting people to confess stuff. That and he liked her company. How could she say no to an offer like that? Plus, she got to collect some great quotes for the series of articles she was writing on the explosive murder case.

As they rode along the streets of Hampton Cove, which were slowly coming alive again after a short night, she sat slumped down in the passenger seat while he expertly maneuvered his pickup through traffic. "So did you get that report from the fire marshals?"

"We did, actually," he said, looking as cool and collected as ever. Not much ruffled this man, which was probably what made him so good at his job. And in her bed.

"And was nitroglycerin involved?" she prompted.

"Yes, it was. A whole lot of the stuff. And it did come in a beer bottle, as they suspected. But when they checked Curt Pigott's room they found nothing. Not a trace. Not on his person, not on his clothes, not on any of his possessions. Which makes this a very puzzling case."

"And, like he said, why would he use room service to deliver a bomb to his rival? That would make him the dumbest killer in history," she mused as she gazed out the window at the streets outside, where people were walking their children to school and others were hurrying to get to work on time. "So what about the others?"

Chase shook his head. "Nothing. All the interesting men were cleared."

"Someone must have had a bottle of nitroglycerin in their room."

"Someone sure did. Only we haven't been able to find it. Yet. The thing is, this particular nitro was homemade, not factory-made, which tells us a few things."

He used his indicator to turn left onto Main Street. As usual, there wasn't a single parking spot left in front of the hotel, so he turned the car down the ramp and into the parking garage reserved for hotel guests.

"Whoever mixed the nitro must have done so where they wouldn't be disturbed. Because nitro is a notoriously unstable substance, and tends to explode when you don't know what you're doing. Plus, nitro has some serious side effects."

"Like?"

"It affects the arteries, widening them, which is why it's so useful against heart conditions and chest pains. The side effect is that it opens the blood vessels in the brain, too, which can cause some serious headaches. They call it NG head, or bang head, and it's more like a migraine than a mild headache. Other side effects are dizziness, nausea, flushing…"

"So we're looking for a killer with a serious case of migraine."

"Or those migraines could have passed by the time he or she came to Hampton Cove. It's the fumes and working with the stuff that's tricky. Once it's transferred into a canister and kept on ice it's much safer to handle."

"On ice?"

"Oh, yes. Nitro is notoriously unstable. One wrong move and boom! So it's handled at low temperatures and stored that way, too."

She sighed. "So we're looking for a killer who may or may not have had headaches in the past and who used a cold bottle of beer to kill the Most Fascinating Man in the World."

Chase gave her a grin. "Isn't this the most fascinating case you've ever worked on?"

They got out of the car and rode the elevator up to the lobby. The four men they were here to interview were waiting in the conference room. For the sake of expedience Chase had decided to interview them together instead of one by one. And so it was that when they walked into the conference room, the Most Intriguing, Most Iconic, Most Attractive and Sexiest Men in the World were seated around the table, drumming their fingers and looking glum and annoyed.

Most interesting men don't like to be kept waiting. And they don't appreciate jumping through hoops to satisfy the members of law enforcement.

What was more, Odelia had the distinct impression there was tension in the air. She could be mistaken, but she thought these men didn't like each other very much.

Chase came straight down to business. "All of you guys had both motive and opportunity to stage an attack on Burt Goldsmith. What I would like to know is who you think is responsible for what happened to him."

He pulled back a chair and took a seat, and Odelia followed suit.

The men all shared suspicious glances, but Bobbie Hawe was the first to speak. The Most Attractive Man in the World was a handsome fortysomething male of powerful build who obviously spent a great deal of time in the gym. He was dressed in a three-piece suit that was filled out by a muscular physique, and sported the kind of well-groomed facial hair that Robert Downey Jr. was so fond of. He also wore that actor's favored tinted glasses.

"I know what you're doing and it won't work, detective," he said in a low drawl.

"Oh? And what is it you think I'm doing?" asked Chase.

"You're trying to pit us against each other. Make us roll over and give you the name of the culprit." He spread his arms. "And I *would* give you the name of the culprit. If I knew."

There were murmurs of agreement from his fellow interesting men.

"It's not a big secret that none of us are great friends," Bobbie continued, "but that doesn't mean we aim to kill each other or blow each other up. And we definitely would never have tried to kill Burt Goldsmith, who was the elder statesman of our select group."

"We have it on good authority that Burt came down to Hampton Cove to steal attention away from your conference," said Odelia.

Bobbie laughed. "Let me guess. Curt told you that, right?" She nodded.

"He wasn't lying. Burt did come down here out of spite. But that doesn't mean there was no mutual respect. We're all businessmen, detective—Miss Poole. We compete for the same share of the market. But above all we respected Burt. For what he'd accomplished. And for his stamina. I mean, the man was as old as my grandfather—and still going strong."

"Burt was a legend," chimed in Jasper Hanson, Most

Intriguing Man in the World. He was small and physically negligible, but there was something about him that was most... intriguing. Maybe it was his face, which didn't seem put together well. His eyes too far apart, his lips too thin. His nose too flat. Whatever the case, when he spoke, everyone listened. "I actually liked the man," he continued, ignoring howls of protest from his colleagues. "No, I really did. We had a connection. We would meet each other on the road—us interesting men do a lot of trade shows and conventions, as you might imagine—or in some hotel bar, and we would invariably drift into each other's ken, sharing a few beers—bourbon for him. Burt didn't like the taste of beer, not even his own brand—and swap war stories." His expression sobered. "He will be sorely missed by this community. And definitely by yours truly."

"I never liked him," said Nestor Greco, the Most Iconic Man in the World. He was squat, heavyset, with receding hairline, and dressed head to foot in black. He looked like a guy who could have had a part in *Goodfellas*, shooting the breeze with the local mobsters. "I thought he was a fake. Just a big phony."

"Burt was the real deal," said Jasper. "The most interesting man of all."

"Nah, he wasn't. He was an actor playing a part. The real Burt was a bore and a drunk. A drunk!" he insisted over the protestations of his colleague. "The only time he was interesting was when he was drunk as a skunk—but then we're all interesting when we're plastered. Even the biggest dullard in the world becomes interesting when he's loaded to the gills."

"I think you're all wrong," said Dale Parson, the Sexiest Man Alive. He looked like a swimwear model, with his sharp features, wavy blond hair and piercing blue eyes. "The only one who ever knew Burt the man was me. I never told anyone this but he's the one who got me launched in this business. I was a walk-on on one of his commercials when he spotted me and gave me my first big break. Hooked me up with his ad campaign manager and that's how I got started modeling swimwear for Vic's Secret and underwear for Kevin Klein." He tapped the table smartly. "That's the kind of guy Burt was. Generous and loyal to his friends."

"So who killed him?" asked Chase. "If all of you thought he was so great—"

"I never said he was great," said Nestor. "I said he was a loser."

"You said he was a bore," Jasper corrected him.

"A bore and a loser. And a drunk. A nasty drunk. He once got into a fight with a nun. A nun! Who gets into a fight with a holy woman? Only a drunk loser like Burt Goldsmith!"

"Don't call him a loser," said Dale, looking pained. "Burt was like a father to me."

"Well, maybe he *was* your father," said Nestor.

"What are you saying? That Burt screwed my mother?" asked Dale, rising.

"That's exactly what I'm saying! Burt screwed everyone's mother and *their* mother!"

"Please, gentlemen," said Bobbie. "Let's not do this. A man died. Show some respect."

"He never had any respect for me!" said Nestor. "Why should I show respect for a man who wiped his ass on my profession! Wiped his ass on me!"

"Please," Bobbie repeated. "Is this helpful? Is this productive? Please."

"The man was an asswipe," Nestor continued, "and he screwed your mother," he told Dale, pointing his finger at the man. "Which makes you an asswipe's asswipe!"

The veins in the swimwear model's temples were throbbing, and his fists were clenched. It wouldn't take much for him to take a swing at the squat Nestor Greco.

"Please," Bobbie said again. "This is not the way we do things around here."

"This is exactly the way we do things around here," said Jasper softly, squinting at the ceiling, a nickel playing through his fingers. "Which is why we'll all get arrested and charged with first-degree murder if we don't get our acts together and figure out who's behind this."

"Well, we all know who's behind this, don't we?" said Nestor.

"If you're going to say my mother is behind this, I'll slug you," said Dale. "I swear to god I'll slug you and I'll slug you good and proper."

"Asswipes don't slug people," Nestor pointed out. "They—"

"Don't say it," Dale warned. "Don't you dare!"

"I suggest you take a long hard look at Tracy Sting, detective," said Jasper. "We might not agree on anything, but we all agree on this. Tracy is the one who did this to Burt."

"Tracy Sting?" asked Odelia. "Who is she?"

"Burt's handler," said Chase. "We've been wanting to have a word with her."

"Tracy represents Dos Siglas," said Bobbie. "Like you said, she's the one who handled Burt. Organized the shoots with the ad company. Scheduled his appearances."

"So why would she kill the goose that laid the golden eggs?" asked Chase.

All four men were silent for a moment, sharing glances. Even Nestor turned quiet, and Dale had taken a seat again. None of them spoke, as if in sudden agreement.

"Gentlemen?" Chase prompted.

"Look, Burt was old, all right?" said Bobbie. "The man was past his prime. But he didn't think about hanging up his saddle. Said he still had at least a dozen good years left in him. Which would have put him past ninety. Now I'm all against ageism, detective, but ninety? Seriously? So Dos Siglas wanted to put him out to pasture. Replace him with a younger model. Maybe even change up the campaign a little. A fresh take, you know."

"Burt wouldn't accept their offer," Jasper chimed in. "He refused to stand down. Said that if they forced him to retire he'd take them to court. Sue them for all they were worth."

"In their eagerness to sign him up, back in the day, they'd forgotten to stipulate a termination clause," Bobbie explained. "So Burt figured he would go on in perpetuity."

"And they couldn't fire him for fear of bad press," said Nestor.

"So they killed him?" asked Odelia. "Just like that?"

"Why not?" said Jasper. "It was their only out. And a lot of free publicity, too." He leaned in. "Imagine the headlines: Most Fascinating Man in the World dies in a Most Fascinating Way. By exploding beer bottle. The articles write themselves. Not to mention that they planted a Tres Siglas bottle at the scene, smearing the competition in the process." He leaned back. "From an adman's point of view the death of Burt Goldsmith was a golden opportunity. A master stroke. And Tracy Sting is the person who set the whole thing up."

CHAPTER 22

*A*lec Lip sat nursing his beer while gazing out the window at one of the most interesting sights in the world: the people who inhabited Hampton Cove. They were his fellow citizens, the people he was being paid to protect and serve, but also his friends, co-workers, family members and former fellow schoolmates. Above all, though, they were people, and people watching was one of Alec's favorite pastimes. Better than a movie at the local cineplex. Better than a show on Netflix or one of the networks. And definitely better than sitting at home and wondering if Chase would stay over at Odelia's tonight or not.

Last night he'd hoped to catch a game with the guy, but as usual he'd been a no-show. Not that he minded all that much. Most nights they both ate dinner at the Pooles anyway, and often hung out at Marge and Tex's while Chase snuck over next door to canoodle with Alec's niece. Was it still canoodling when you were past the legal drinking age? He wasn't sure. At any rate, there would be many more ball games, and if Chase was serious about Odelia—and it looked that way to Alec—the guy would become family, which was all for the good, cause he liked Chase. Liked him like a brother. Or the son he never had.

And he was just putting the beer bottle to his lips again when a tall and striking redhead loomed up in his field of vision and jutted out a shapely hip. Shapely was the word that described the rest of her as well. From her well-pronounced chest to a pair of legs that seemed to stretch on for miles, a face that could have launched a thousand ships, and luxuriant curly hair the color of burnished copper. The woman was all woman, top to toe, and dressed the way he liked, too: checkered shirt, tight jeans, cowboys boots. Howdy, sister!

"Is this seat taken, sheriff?" she asked in a sexily hoarse voice.

"No, ma'am, it sure ain't," he heard himself reply.

She drew out a chair and sat down across from him, fixing him with the greenest pair of eyes he'd ever seen. A tickle ran up his spine, and the world seemed to hold its breath.

"Sheriff Alec Lip, right?"

He was nodding before he realized that he wasn't a sheriff at all. "Chief Lip," he managed, and noticed he was holding onto that bottle of beer as if it were a lifeline. She was that kind of woman.

"Chief Lip," she amended.

"Though folks around here just call me Chief Alec."

She smiled, and the sun suddenly seemed to shine just that little bit brighter. "My name is Tracy Sting, Chief. I heard you were looking for me?"

He controlled himself with a powerful effort. "As a matter of fact I was, Miss Sting."

She threw out her hands and settled in. "Well, here I am. Ask away, Chief Alec."

Her voice had that Demi Moore grit, as if she'd been

smoking a pack a day since the cradle. Hard to imagine a woman like this ever having been in the cradle, though. More likely she'd been born fully formed. He cleared his foggy mind and his throat. "You were Burt Goldsmith's go-to-person for everything Dos Siglas, is that correct?"

"That is correct. I work for the company, and assigned to Burt as his personal assistant and executive contact. Whatever Burt needed, I got him."

He arched an eyebrow. "Everything?"

She glanced at him from beneath lowered lashes. "Everything."

He decided to ignore the innuendo. "And is it also correct that Dos Siglas were aiming to get rid of Burt but his contract wouldn't allow them?"

She smiled a tight smile. "Who told you that?"

"I'm a cop, Miss Sting. It's my job to know these things." That and the message Chase had just sent him. Apparently his and Odelia's interview had pointed to Tracy as the killer.

She shrugged. "I guess it's not a big secret. It's true that Burt signed an ironclad contract that allowed him to stay on long after what most people would consider the age of retirement. And it's also true that Dos Siglas had naturally assumed that Burt would call it quits once he reached the mid-seventies. He didn't, however, and felt that as long as his health allowed, he would keep going. The man was having too much fun, Chief. He wasn't going to quit the best job in the world just because some company figurehead said so."

He played with his bottle for a moment. "Did you try to persuade him to quit?"

There was some fire in those eyes now. "No, I did not. I thought he was doing a damn good job. The man might have been older than my father but he was fitter than most men his age and in better shape than a lot of men a lot younger than him. Plus, the public loved him." She leaned in and tapped the table between them. "Burt Goldsmith sold more beer than anyone that's ever lived, just by being himself: a funny, charming, sweet old guy." She leaned back. "If he wanted to go on until he dropped dead, who was I to stop him?"

"Someone stopped him. Permanently," he pointed out.

"Well, it wasn't me, and it wasn't anyone at Dos Siglas. The bosses wanted out of the contract, sure, but that doesn't mean they were going to blow up their best investment. Can you imagine the shitstorm that would come down on us if it turns out we blew up our most popular pitchman? Burt *was* Dos Siglas. He was the face of the company." She shook her head, her red mane provocatively dangling around those slender shoulders. "No, Chief. Someone fed you some wrong information. Someone else killed Burt and I, for one, want to see this person punished to the full extent of the law. Maybe even more than you do."

"I very much doubt that," he said, and was rewarded with an icy look. Ouch.

"You think I did this? Blow up my charge and risk my reputation and freedom?"

"I'm sure your company will reward you handsomely for your work—and provide you with future opportunities even more lucrative than babysitting Burt Goldsmith."

She smoldered for a moment, then laughed, a throaty sound that was very pleasant. "I like you, Chief Alec Lip. You're direct. You say it like it is. And I can see that you've already made up your mind about me." She rose from her chair in one fluid motion. "You think I'm a killer. A stone-cold murderess."

"I wouldn't go so far as that," he protested. "I merely wanted to point out that—"

"No, you're absolutely right," she said. "I am the perfect

suspect. Which means I'll have to convince you that you're wrong about me. What about dinner and a movie?"

Alec's brows shot up. Now this was a first. First time a woman asked *him* out on a date. And first time since his Ginny died that he was actually considering saying yes. Before he could think things through, Tracy Sting gave him a knowing nod. "Pick me up at eight. Room 433. And don't be late, Chief. If there's anything that turns me off it's tardiness." And then she was off, swinging those hips and turning the head of every guy in the establishment.

Alec shook his own head, feeling dizzy and dazed. What had just happened? And then he was getting up from his chair and moving after her. "Wait up, Miss Sting—Tracy!"

CHAPTER 23

*O*nce again Dooley and I were on the move. Even though the weight of woe pressed down upon us in the form of Dooley's potential move to Colorado, we'd decided not to let it worry us too much. Cats are a notoriously resilient species. Not only because of the fact that we have nine lives instead of the measly single one humans have been allotted, but also because we always tend to land on our paws. What was more, Dooley had been blessed with a great idea. If this Most Fascinating Cat in the World had run off and taken to the streets, who better to track him down than Clarice, our feral friend, who owned these very streets?

And so it was that the new day saw us traipsing along the back alleys of Hampton Cove, dumpster diving and searching high and low for the wild cat that was Clarice.

"I hope we find her," remarked Dooley after we'd scoured our third dumpster that morning. "I don't feel up to the long hike out into the woods, Max."

"Me neither," I admitted.

When Clarice isn't looking for scrumptious and tasty bits in Hampton Cove's many dumpsters, she's scrounging off

NIC SAINT

whatever bestselling scribe is occupying Hetta Fried's writer's lodge, which is inconveniently located a goodish bit away from the heart of town.

What with the flea thing and last night's #pillgate and Dooley's sad prospects, I wasn't feeling up to going on a country ramble in the hopes of locating this Shadow feline. I'm prepared to do a lot for my human, but one has to draw the line somewhere, right?

And we were just checking out one of the more dingy back alleys—yes, even a Hamptons haven like Hampton Cove has them—and thumping our paws against the line of dumpsters, caroling, "Clarice, oh, Clari-iece!" like some latter-day Hannibal Lecter wannabes, when suddenly a loud growl sounded and one of the dumpsters spoke back.

"Oh, will you cut it out already?" the dumpster snarled, and I recognized the unmistakable dulcet tones of our favorite wild cat. "You'll wear out my name. Not to mention scare away the tastiest rats!"

"Rats!" cried Dooley. "I don't like rats, Max!"

"Relax. She's just kidding. Aren't you, Clarice?" I said, louder.

The head of a mangy cat appeared at the top of the dumpster and she jumped down, her fur matted and dotted with bald spots, part of one ear gnawed off and more than a few whiskers missing. Clarice jumped down and started washing her face, giving us nasty glances between licks. "You two look like crap. What have you done to yourselves? Gotten stuck in a wood chipper?" She laughed at her own joke, a series of low and throaty chuckles.

"We need your help, Clarice," Dooley announced.

"Of course you do." She then narrowed her eyes at me. "Is that... a collar?"

I cringed. I'd hoped the topic wouldn't crop up. But of course Clarice's eagle eyes had immediately spotted the anomaly. "We've been suffering from a slight flea issue," I said.

She laughed a hacking laugh. "Flea issue! That's why you look so ragged!"

"It's no laughing matter," Dooley said. "It's a terrible ordeal, Clarice. Painful."

"Painful! You don't know what pain is, city cat," she growled, getting in Dooley's face. "Pain is when you take a punch to the gut from a twenty-pound cat with razors for claws. Pain is when a human steps on your tail and grinds it into the ground. Pain is when your own human throws you off a cliff and leaves you to die!" She was panting from the outburst.

We both stared at her, aghast. "Is that what happened to you?" I asked.

She produced a growling sound at the back of her throat, and for a moment I thought she would lunge at me. Instead, she said, "Never get attached to your human. They *will* turn their backs on you. And they *will* leave you to rot and die, alone in the middle of nowhere."

Cheerful. Life around Clarice is always a feast of careless laughs and cheerfulness.

"Is it true that your human left you tied to a tree trunk and that you had to gnaw off your own paw to free yourself?" asked Dooley in a reverent voice.

Involuntarily we glanced at Clarice's paws. She seemed to possess all four of them.

"Oh, who cares," snarled Clarice. "That's all ancient history anyway."

Just then, a flea jumped from Dooley in the direction of the feral cat. Clarice snatched it up in midair, then flicked it into her mouth and chomped down. "Not a lot of meat," she grumbled. "Got any more?"

I gulped. "You're not afraid they'll suck your blood?"

She laughed. "A flea suck my blood! I suck their blood! That's why they never come near me."

I had noticed she wasn't wearing a collar. Then again, if her human was the kind of person to throw her off a cliff to leave her to die and rot, he probably wouldn't take her to Vena's for flea treatment. "You don't have fleas?" I asked.

"Do you see a flea on me?" she asked, and I had to admit I didn't. Fleas were probably more afraid of Clarice than she was of the little parasites. "Now are you gonna tell me what you want or are you gonna stand there yapping about your sad little lives?"

"We're looking for Shadow," said Dooley.

"Look behind you. But be quick," she quipped.

Dooley did look behind him, then back at Clarice. "I don't get it," he said.

"Not *our* shadow," I clarified. "Shadow. She's the Most Fascinating Cat in the World, and she's gone missing. She belonged to the Most Fascinating Man in the World but he got blown up, and if we can find her we want to ask her if she saw who killed her human."

"Good riddance," Clarice grunted. "I would blow up my human if I had the chance."

"Who was your human, Clarice?" asked Dooley, interested.

In response, she merely gave him a dirty look. "I've seen Shadow," she said. "Seen her rooting around my dumpsters, looking for scraps. Sad little creature. Namby-pamby cat. Scurrying away into the shadows like the kind of thing you find when you turn over a rock."

"Where have you seen her?" I asked, my heart lifting with hope and excitement.

Clarice gestured vaguely. "Around. You'll have to hurry, though. Cat looked absolutely mangy. Mangy and derelict. Wouldn't surprise me if she's dead by now." She nodded knowingly. "It takes a special kind of cat to survive on these mean streets, boys. Trust me when I tell you these streets are unforgiving and they are relentless. No place for sissy cats like you. Or Shadow." She gave us a stern look. "Just giving it to you straight. No fairy tales. That way you won't be disappointed when you come upon her emaciated, rat-infested, maggot-crawling carcass in a gutter on the edge of town, nothing but a piece of road kill."

Like I said, time spent with Clarice is always a joy to the heart and balm to the soul.

CHAPTER 24

The interview with the four remaining most interesting men concluded, Odelia decided to swing by the house for a bite to eat. Chase dropped her off and continued on to the station house, wanting to discuss the case with Uncle Alec. And she'd just inserted her key in the door and stepped inside when she became aware that she wasn't alone.

Someone else was in there with her, and it wasn't Max or Dooley.

"Who's there?" she called out, afraid some burglar had decided to go for her meager belongings. They wouldn't find much to satisfy their thieving tastes. Unless they were fellow cat owners and excited by the prospect of getting their kibble in bulk at the local Walmart or Costco, they'd be sorely disappointed by their sad little haul.

She took a firm hold on the baseball bat she liked to keep next to the front door—one of Chase's contributions to interior decorating—and took a tentative step. Her house was a smallish affair, and from her position in the hallway she had a good view of the living room, the kitchen, and even the backyard through the sliding glass doors. Just then, the stairs creaked, and she gasped. Someone *was* in here! Score one for the Poole survival instinct.

"Show yourself!" she yelled. "I'm armed and extremely dangerous!"

She lifted the baseball bat, wondering if she was holding it right and also wondering if she'd have both the time and the gumption to take a swing at this daytime intruder.

Just then, a person came stomping down the stairs and she raised the bat over her head. "I'm—I'm not kidding!" she cried. "I've got a weapon and I'm not afraid to use it!"

"Where do you keep the sheets?" asked Grandma, stepping out from the stairwell and giving her a look of annoyance. She frowned when she saw Odelia's Babe Ruth imitation. "So this is what you get up to when I'm not looking. Having fun and playing games. And they wonder why this generation is so soft." She shook her head and headed into the kitchen, opening the fridge. "And nothing to eat, of course. Sad. Very sad."

"Gran," Odelia cried, lowering her deadly weapon. "What are you doing here?"

"I'm moving in," announced her grandmother, extracting a carton of eggs from the fridge and a tomato. "Don't you have bacon? I need bacon if I'm gonna get through this. Bacon has always been my comfort food of choice."

"But-but-but," she sputtered.

Grandma plunked her bony frame down on a high kitchen stool and planted her elbows on the counter. "I got canned," she said. "Got called out as a fraud and a cheat."

Odelia stared at her grandmother. "I don't get it."

"Neither do I. Things were going great. Philippe was really taking to me, I could tell. Calling me Granny Goldsmith and stuff, and showing me pictures from when he was a baby. He didn't even mention Scarlett Canyon anymore—

having seen right through the woman I'll bet." She puckered up her face. "And then *she* showed up and ruined the whole thing."

"She?" asked Odelia, also taking a seat at the kitchen counter.

"Sure. She. Amelia Goldsmith she calls herself. Burt's wife. Turns out Burt may have played the part of the player, cutting a neat swath through a pack of blond bimbos over the years, but all this time the guy was married, can you believe it? Married! And to the same woman, no less. Claims she's the mother of Burt's boy Hunter and Philippe is her grandson."

"But what about the DNA test?"

"Results came back. Neither me nor Scarlett made the cut. Nope," she said, heaving an unhappy sigh. "Looks like that ship has sailed. Burt and I may have done the horizontal mambo back in the day, but ne'er a son was born from our union. And the same goes for the Canyon menace, though I could have told you this without some stupid darned DNA test."

"So… that means you're staying put?"

"Sure." Gran slapped the counter and got up. "So where are those sheets? And you know I like them light and fluffy. None of that flannel stuff. I've got sensitive skin."

She gave her grandparent a look of confusion. "What do you need sheets for? Don't you have plenty of sheets at your own place?"

Gran's face darkened. "I don't have a place. Marge and Tex are dead to me. No way am I going back to those two backstabbers. After the way they treated me? Not one ounce of support for my bid to become Granny Goldsmith and rake in the millions." She shook her head decidedly. "Nah-uh. I'm moving in with you." She spread her arms. "Granny's home!"

CHAPTER 25

*W*e met up with Brutus and Harriet on the corner of Main Street and Franklin Avenue. Brutus and Harriet had formed a second team to look for Shadow. It was obvious from their expressions that they hadn't found what they were looking for either, though.

"Did you find her?" asked Brutus.

"No, did you?" asked Dooley, who had a hard time reading faces.

"We did find Clarice," I told the others. "She said she saw Shadow and that if we don't hurry it might be too late."

Brutus frowned. "You mean she might have left town?"

"She might have left the planet."

"As in... flown off into space?"

"As in being dead and buried."

"Look, all this talk about Shadow is all well and good," said Harriet, "but shouldn't we focus on the more important issue here?"

We all stared at her. "What more important issue?" I asked.

She tapped her collar. "These, of course! When are we

going to be allowed to get rid of these horrible collars? Cats are staring at us, in case you hadn't noticed. Mocking us."

I looked around. Every single cat I saw was also wearing a collar, and they weren't staring, either, too busy wallowing in self-pity, just like Harriet was. Cats are notoriously self-absorbed, and Harriet is a prime example. It's one of our less attractive qualities, I'm afraid.

"I guess once the fleas are gone the collar can come off," I said.

"Duh. In case you hadn't noticed, the fleas *are* gone," said Harriet. "So you better talk to Odelia and get her to remove these terrible things ASAP, Max. And better do it now."

"I saw a flea," Dooley piped up. "It jumped from me to Clarice but then she ate it."

Harriet ignored this outburst from one she considered a mere cypher in our small cat universe. "Talk to Odelia, Max. I'm serious."

"Why don't you talk to her?" I asked.

"Because she only listens to you. Everyone knows that."

"That's not true." They all looked at me. "Is it?"

"It is kinda true, Max," Dooley said. "You seem to be her favorite."

"Odelia doesn't have favorites. She loves us all equally."

"Yeah, right," Brutus grunted. "You know that ain't true, Max."

And as we walked on, idly looking left and right for Shadow, I thought about this. Was I Odelia's favorite? I didn't think so. I was her cat, of course. Harriet was Marge's. Dooley was Grandma's, and Brutus was Chase's mom's. But that didn't mean anything. No, I was pretty sure they were mistaken. Odelia loved us all to bits. And we'd just crossed into yet another back alley, when we came upon a strange sight: a man and a woman in a police cruiser were also loving each other to bits. Literally. And they had the steamed-up windows to prove it.

And as we stood watching, mouths agape, I suddenly noticed the guy inside the police cruiser looked awfully familiar. He was portly, with a big head and red sideburns.

Brutus had noticed, too. "Isn't that... Uncle Alec?" he asked.

"No way," said Dooley. "Uncle Alec would never do... what is he doing, exactly?"

A hand suddenly slapped against the window, as the woman appeared to straddle Uncle Alec. And then the car began moving in a curious rhythm, tires squeaking audibly.

I gulped a little, and felt compelled to place my paw over Dooley's eyes, just like one would when suddenly an adult scene pops up in an otherwise family-friendly movie on TV.

"What is she doing to him, Max?" asked Dooley, panicky. "She's choking him!"

"No, she's not."

"But she's on top of him!"

"Brutus, tell him," I said. "Explain to him what's going on. Brutus?"

I glanced around and saw that Brutus and Harriet had moved away and were now ensconced behind a dumpster, engaged in a similar activity as Uncle Alec and the mystery woman inside the car. Probably inspired by the moment. It was hard to make out the woman's features, because of the steamed-up windows, but I could tell she had red hair and was a lot prettier than Uncle Alec. She also seemed to be enjoying herself tremendously, as she was yelling, "Oh, yes, sheriff! Oh, yes, sheriff! Oh, yessss! Sheriff!" It was a little repetitive but Alec didn't seem to mind.

From their perch behind the dumpster, meanwhile, Harriet was yelling, "Oh, yes, Brutus! Oh, yes, Brutus! Oh, yesssss! Brutus!" Obvious plagiarism, of course, but who cared?

"What's happening, Max?" cried Dooley, perfectly disoriented.

I led him away from the scene, my paw still over his eyes. "Nothing special," I told him. "Let's go. I think I saw Shadow."

"Is that Harriet? What is she yelling about? Is she in pain?"

I glanced back at Harriet, whose face was contorted in rapture. "I don't think so."

"Because she sounds like she's in pain."

"I'm sure she's fine, Dooley. Brutus will take care of her."

And Brutus was taking care of her. And finding the time to give me two paws up. Guess Vena's vitamin pills had worked their magic after all. I held up one paw in greeting, my other paw protecting Dooley's innocence, and then we were out on the street, where life was lived at a less strenuous pace and public displays of indecency were not as prevalent.

Like I said, sometimes being a cat is tough. Not as tough as Clarice seems to believe, but not something for pussies, either.

We hadn't found Shadow, but Brutus had found his catliness, Uncle Alec had found a woman who didn't seem to mind that he was overweight and out of shape, and I had found that sometimes helping friends was all about chomping down pills that aren't necessarily good for you, and helping other friends by pretending a couple in heat is just another feature of small-town life. Nothing to see here, folks. Just move along. Which is exactly what we did.

CHAPTER 26

Odelia listened to the ringing tone once, twice, three times—and wondered why her uncle wasn't picking up his phone. This was the third time she tried to call him and each time she got his voicemail. Normally he picked up on the first ring so where was he?

She tried Chase instead, who did pick up on the first ring.

"Hey, babe," he said, his new favorite word for her. She could get used to it.

"Have you seen my uncle? He's not picking up his phone."

"Nope. Isn't at the station, either. No idea where he is, actually. Why?"

"I have a situation here. With his mother."

"Uh-oh. What has she gone and done now?"

"She's moved in with me."

Silence. Then: "I think I misheard. Did you say she moved in?"

"Yup. The Goldsmith gambit backfired and since Mom and Dad didn't support her claim to fame and fortune she decided to move out of their house and into mine."

"Um…"

"I know we said you'd move in, but considering this new situation, maybe we should reconsider?"

"I can wait. How long before she moves back out?"

"A week. Tops."

"Don't tell me. This isn't the first time."

"Last time she moved out was because Dad made her wash the dishes. She told him she wasn't his flunky and Dad told her he wasn't her houseboy and things kind of escalated from there. Took them a week to make nice again and for things to return to normal."

"I can wait a week."

"You can still sleep over."

"With Granny breathing heavily in the next room? I don't think so."

"I thought nothing could turn you off?"

"Honey, the thing that can turn me off still has to be born or invented, but I draw the line at getting hot and heavy with my girlfriend while her grandmother hovers over the bed with a curious expression on her face. Call me a prude but exhibitionism isn't my thing."

As she disconnected the thought occurred to her that this would put a serious crimp in her love life. Then her mind returned to Tracy Sting, the woman who was now their prime suspect in the Burt Goldsmith murder. From what the four most interesting men had told them the woman could hold her own as a gunslinger as well as possessing a black belt in all the known martial arts forms as well as a few she'd never even heard about. Armed and dangerous, Chase had called her, and had told his fellow officers to keep a lookout for the woman. Chances were that Burt's killer had been right under their noses all along.

She moved upstairs to help her grandmother settle in—or convince her to move out. When she found the old lady bouncing up and down on the bed in the guest bedroom, she abandoned that particular hope. Granny Muffin looked like she was ready to make her granddaughter's home her new permanent home away from home.

"Did you find the sheets?" she asked, then saw that Gran had. Her finest pink ones, no less. The ones with the Hello Kitty theme. The ones she'd put away when Chase started staying over. Nothing acts as a natural testosterone repellent like Hello Kitty pink does.

"I found a male toothbrush in the bathroom," Gran announced sternly.

How she would distinguish a male toothbrush from a female one Odelia did not know. As far as she knew toothbrushes were genderless. Nevertheless she blushed.

"It's possible Chase has been staying over once or twice."

Gran cocked her head. "Honey, I don't want to interfere with your love life."

Hope surged.

"So whenever you guys feel horny just tell me and I'll put in my earplugs."

Hope crashed.

"How long will you be staying?" she asked, braving Granny's ire.

"Forever by the looks of things." She glanced around at the guest bedroom, a small affair in comparison to Gran's own room next door. "I like it here. I think I'll be very happy. Do you have a VCR? I don't want to miss my favorite shows. I like to tape them just in case."

"VCR went out the window when the world went digital, Gran."

Gran's eyes went wide. "I'm gonna miss my shows? I can't miss my shows!"

"Relax. I've got DVR, and so has Dad."

"Yeah, ask for instructions. He's got all the deets. He's been taping my stuff forever." A cloud momentarily passed over her face, and her dentures dug into her lower lip at the mention of her son-in-law. The moment passed and then she was strong again. "Better yet, ask Alec. He'll know what to do. At least Alec never kicked me out of his home."

"You never lived in Alec's home, Gran."

"That's what I meant," she said vaguely, then bounced up from the bed. "Now show me how to work the shower. I like it not too hot, not too cold, and Tex never moves the mixer tap. I hate it when people move the mixer tap. Pisses me off big time."

And as Odelia followed her grandmother into the bathroom, she discovered a newfound appreciation for her mother and father's predicament. She'd lived with her grandmother for all of half an hour and already she was contemplating geronticide.

CHAPTER 27

e were finally on our way home, having struck out in our mission to find Burt's Shadow. Dooley kept harping on about Uncle Alec and Harriet and Brutus for a while but then fell into a contemplative silence. Which suited me just fine. I had my own thoughts to contend with. It might surprise you but cats are deep thinkers. And so it was that when Dooley finally spoke again, it was to launch into a train of thought that took me by surprise.

"Maybe we should get girlfriends, Max."

I was slightly taken aback. "Girlfriends? What do you mean?"

"Like Uncle Alec and that mystery woman in the car. Or Brutus and Harriet." He shrugged. "Everybody has a girl-friend. Even Uncle Alec has a girlfriend. What about Shanille? You like Shanille, don't you? And she can sing. Who doesn't want a girlfriend who can sing?"

The thought of Father Reilly's homely tabby didn't stir any of those finer feelings in me that one associates with eternal love and affection and I told Dooley in no uncertain terms that never in my life would I want to find myself in a passionate embrace with Shanille.

"Then who, Max? There has to be a Molly out there for us somewhere, right?"

Frankly I hadn't given the matter as much thought as Dooley obviously had. Which just goes to show. Still waters sometimes do run deep. Or is it shallow waters? No matter.

"Look, if the right one is out there for us, one day we'll find her. Or she'll find us."

He gave me a look of hope. "You think so?"

"I know so." Actually I didn't, but the topic of conversation was not one on which I cared to dwell at the moment.

"What about Clarice?"

"What about her?"

"Doesn't she make your heart go pitter-patter?"

Clarice did make my heart go pitter-patter, but that was probably because she scared the living daylights out of me. "Not really. Why? Do you like her?"

He gave this serious consideration. "I admire her. I think she's great. But I don't see her in a romantic light. Not like Richard Gere saw Julia at the end of *Pretty Woman*. Or all those couples in *Love Actually*. Though I do think that one day Clarice will find love again."

"Again? You think she found it before?"

That was a toughie, and he was lost in thought once more. When he finally emerged, it was to address a different topic altogether. "Maybe I should take one of those pills."

I looked up in alarm. "Pills? What pills?"

"The ones you and Brutus took. It's obvious they did you a lot of good."

"They made us puke our guts out."

"And then they made you find love."

"I didn't find love."

"You found Clarice—and I do think she likes you, Max. The way she was looking at you just now."

"She called me a sissy cat!"

"I'm sure she meant it as a compliment." He sighed wistfully. "My one true love will come to me once I take those pills. I'm sure about that now."

Good thing Odelia threw those pills in the trash. We'd arrived home and traipsed in through the cat door Odelia had her dad and uncle and Chase install in the kitchen. Yes, it had taken three men to install one little door. Yours truly had gotten stuck in the first iteration, and the next ones, but the current version was one size fits all—even my size.

To our surprise Grandma was seated on the sofa, watching one of her daytime soaps.

"Gran? What are you doing here?" I asked upon seeing the crusty old lady.

"Watching television. What does it look like I'm doing?" she said without looking away from a couple of overly handsome doctors chatting up a couple of overly pretty female patients.

"Shouldn't you be watching television in your own home?" I asked, having developed a powerful sense of privacy ever since the Brutuses and Chase Kingsleys of this world had started invading my home.

She waved an annoyed hand. "This is my home now. I moved in with my granddaughter."

Dooley and I shared a look of surprise.

"You're not going to Colorado?" asked Dooley, hope surging.

"Nah. The Goldsmiths can have their Colorado. They don't want me—I don't want them. Good riddance." She cast a quick glance down at Dooley. "You look awfully pleased."

Dooley couldn't speak from the emotion clogging up his throat so I decided to speak for him. "Dooley was afraid you were going to take him to Colorado, away from his friends and family."

Grandma frowned, as if she hadn't considered this. "Look, fellas," she said finally, "maybe this whole Goldsmith business wasn't such a bright idea after all. I mean, going to live with one's in-laws can be a terrible nuisance. Just look at me and Tex. What a mess! I swear to God, if that Philippe or any of his ilk had given you or me a hard time, I'd have packed my bags and returned to Hampton Cove just as soon as I had the chance, millions or no millions." She scratched Dooley, who'd jumped up on the couch, behind the ears. "I'd never let anyone talk down to you, my pet. You know that, right? If those people had given you the cold shoulder I'd have told them to go screw themselves. Besides, I'm needed here."

This gave me pause. Needed here? Dooley, too, found this statement odd.

"Needed for what, Gran?" he asked.

One eye on her soap opera and one eye on Dooley, she said vaguely, "Odelia, of course. It's obvious she's gonna need the sage advice of a wise woman like myself."

This could only mean one thing, and Dooley came right out and said it: "Babies?"

"Uh-huh," said Gran absently. A particularly handsome doctor was now nuzzling the neck of a particularly pretty female patient, and so she shushed us when we said more.

Dooley jumped down from the couch and joined me for an impromptu emergency meeting in the kitchen, next to my bowls of filtered water, tasty kibble and prime pâté.

"Gran has moved in," Dooley said, summing up the salient point succinctly.

"Yes, she has," I said, nodding seriously.

"And she just admitted she's here for the babies—plural."

"Yes, she did."

"You know what this means, Max."

"Yes, I do."

"Soon there won't be a place for us here."

"No, there won't."

We shared a look of extreme concern, one thought at the forefront of our minds.

"The pound!" we both bleated.

CHAPTER 28

"Where can she be?" Odelia asked annoyedly. She and Chase had been looking all over for Tracy Sting, but thus far the woman had eluded their dragnet. The rest of the Hampton Cove Police Department, too, had kept a watchful eye—but no luck there either.

They were back at the hotel, seated in the lobby, knowing that sooner or later the woman had to show up there. Her room was empty, that much they knew, and she hadn't been in since right after the explosion that had taken her client's life. So where was she?

"She might have returned home," Chase suggested.

"Columbus, Ohio? Didn't you put out an APB on her?"

"I did, but if she rented a car she might have slipped through."

"Her clothes are in her room. Her luggage. Everything."

"If she's the one that did this she might have left regardless."

Which meant they were wasting precious time in this lobby. It felt as if Odelia had spent days at this hotel already, which actually was partly true. She dug into the bowl with potato-covered peanuts the receptionist had been so kind to put out for them. Probably another bad idea. But they were seriously addictive and she'd always been a nervous eater.

"So did your grandmother get settled in all right?"

She gave Chase an 'are-you-kidding-me' look. "She took my Hello Kitty sheets."

"Uh-oh."

"And then she told me she's going to stay with me permanently. As in for-e-vah."

Now it was his turn to give her the look.

She threw up her hands. "I can't just throw her out, Chase. She's my grandmother."

"We could… all move in together. You, me and Granny. That could be... fun. Right?"

He didn't sound convinced. "You and me and my grandmother. In the same house."

"Why not? How bad can it be?"

"Bad. Very bad." She sighed. "We'll just have to learn to live without, I guess."

"Live without…" He gestured between them. "…this?"

"Uh-huh. She told me something about putting in her earplugs but I wouldn't feel comfortable with my granny in the next room. Like you said, it's something of a turn-off."

"When you put it like that."

"I don't know how Mom and Dad have managed all these years."

"Maybe they never do it?"

She grimaced. "Let's not go there." Imagining her parents like that was an even bigger turn-off than imagining her grandmother in the next room, listening to every noise she and Chase made. Then she brightened. "We could rent a room. Here. At this fine establishment."

He placed an arm around her shoulder. "Or we could do it in my car. Or yours. I'm not picky."

She giggled, snuggling into his arm. "I'd like that. Let's steam up some windows."

Just then, Chase's phone chimed. When he placed it to his ear and listened, he arched an eyebrow, as if what he was hearing was a highly unusual piece of news. After he disconnected the call, he was silent for a few beats.

"Was that the station?" she asked.

He nodded automatically.

"Well, what did they say? Did they find Tracy Sting?"

"Oh, they found her," he said in a toneless voice.

"Well? What are you waiting for? Go interrogate the lady."

"It wasn't just her they found."

"What do you mean? She had an accomplice?"

"You could say that." He seemed to shake something off. "A citizen called in a complaint about a display of public indecency. A couple were going at it inside a stationary vehicle. Going at it with some eagerness I might add. Steamed-up windows and everything."

"Don't tell me. Our Miss Nitro and her mystery accomplice?"

He turned to her. "Miss Nitro and your uncle, actually. Cops were dispatched and found them in flagrante delicto inside Alec's police cruiser—both in a state of undress."

🐾

They walked into the police station, and judging from the looks Dolores, the crusty receptionist, was giving them, by now everyone and their uncle were aware of what had happened. "I can't believe my uncle the police chief would do such a thing," Odelia said.

"I can't believe he'd use the cruiser. Isn't that misappropriation of police property?"

"Who cares about the car? He was canoodling with a felon!"

"Maybe she's one of those femme fatales," he offered. "Those are hard to resist."

They arrived at interview room number one, where the entire Hampton Cove police force stood staring through the little window at the woman locked inside. She was a striking beauty, no doubt about it. Flaming red hair, perfect features, a chest Odelia would have given her eyeteeth for. At least she was dressed, which hadn't been the case when they arrested her, as the arresting officer loudly explained to his fascinated audience.

"Where's my uncle?" asked Odelia.

They all pointed to interview room number two. Odelia took a glance through the window and saw her uncle fuming silently inside, pacing the small space. She grimaced. Awkward. Chase had followed her and placed a hand on her back. "I'll interview the woman first. See what she says. And then I'll deal with your uncle."

She watched as Chase entered the interview room along with a colleague, and folded her arms across her chest. She noticed how every cop standing there with her did the same, all settling in for what promised to be a most entertaining show.

"Miss Sting," said Chase as he took a seat, his colleague, a female officer named Sarah Flunk, rifling through some notes as she shot not-so-friendly glances at the suspect. "Are you aware that there are laws in this state against public lewdness?"

Miss Sting made an annoyed gesture. "We were in a private vehicle parked in a back alley, hidden from view or so we thought. Can I help it if some nosy parker peeping tom pervert do-gooder decided to stick his nose where it doesn't belong? And isn't the chief of police exempt or something?"

Chase coughed into his fist. "Where did you and the Chief meet?"

She leveled an icy look at him. "Why don't you ask him?"

"I'm asking you."

"I met him in a bar. He accused me of being a cold-blooded murderer so I invited him to dinner. That's when he came after me and invited me into his car. Things kinda took off from there." She made a gesture of annoyance. "Look, we're consenting adults, officer—"

"Detective."

"Whatever. None of your business what your boss and I were doing in his car."

"Fine," he said. "Frankly I don't care what you and Chief Alec were doing. What does concern me is that you're the prime suspect in a murder investigation and that your engaging with the person in charge of that investigation amounts to a form of bribery."

She uttered an exclamation. "Bribery? Really? Are you nuts?"

"Insulting a police officer isn't going to—"

"No, really. I already told Alec I didn't have anything to do with this whole Burt Goldsmith thing." She sliced the air with her hand, spitting out the words. "No-*thing*!"

Chase smiled. "Obviously you were most persuasive."

"You're a pig," said the woman, shaking her head.

"And you're in hot water here, lady. We have four witnesses who claim your company hired you to 'take care of' Burt when he wouldn't go quietly into the night. So you decided to release him from his contract with a bang. What did you tell him? You're fired?"

"Oh, please," she said, rolling her eyes. "I guess this is where I tell you I want to speak to my lawyer."

"And this is where I tell you that it won't do you any good."

"Are you going to charge me? If so, go right ahead. If not, I think I'll be leaving now."

"You're not going anywhere, Miss Sting."

All around Odelia, cops were glued to the one-way window, following the back-and-forth with relish. Just then, Odelia's phone chimed and she walked out of the small space and into the corridor. "Yes, Gran?" she said, stepping into her uncle's office for a moment.

"You better get over here," said her grandmother.

"Why? What happened?"

"It's Dooley. He's not well."

Ice suddenly curdled her veins. "I'll be there in ten."

"Come to Vena's. That's where we took him."

CHAPTER 29

$\mathcal{T}$he whole family was gathered at Vena's, hovering around Dooley's sickbed. The scene resembled one plucked straight from one of Grandma's soap operas. Well, minus the beefcake doctor. Instead we had to make do with Vena, not a picture of beauty and grace, unfortunately. Then again, she'd saved Dooley's life, which made her a hero in my book.

"Why the hell did he take those pills?" asked Tex, shaking his white-haired head.

"I just wanted to see what they tasted like," said Dooley in a thin and reedy voice.

"You know what they tasted like," I said. "I told you they tasted horrible. And would more than likely make you puke your guts out."

I'd jumped on top of the cat bed and was keeping my buddy company. I was the one who'd alerted Grandma that something was wrong when I found Dooley passed out on the kitchen floor, unresponsive and pretty much dead to the world. Apparently he'd hopped on the kitchen counter and had gobbled up all the remaining vitamin pills.

"I never should have left those pills out," said Odelia.

"You couldn't have known," said Marge soothingly.

"Who would have thought that vitamins could be bad for you?" said Grandma.

"Some cats have an adverse reaction," Vena said. "If you ingest as many as Dooley did, it causes havoc to the digestive system, which in turn puts pressure on the heart."

"Good thing Max was there to save him," said Grandma. "If not for him, he might have died."

"Thanks for saving my life, Max," said Dooley, smiling weakly.

"Any time, buddy," I said. "Just don't swallow so many pills again, will you? You almost gave *me* heart failure."

Vena left to attend to some of her other patients, and Odelia addressed Dooley directly. Since Chase wasn't here, and it was just family, she could talk freely. "Never do that to me again, all right, little guy? I thought I lost you. You scared the hell out of me."

"I just thought… if you and Chase have those babies—"

"What babies?"

"The babies you and Chase are having. The reason Gran has moved in with us."

The humans all stared at one another. This was obviously news to them.

Dooley gave them a sad look. "There won't be a place for us at your home once those babies arrive, and you'll be forced to take us to the pound. And we all know what life at the pound is like. Not a place for sissy cats like me and Max. A cat needs to be tough to survive life at the pound. Clarice would thrive, but Max and I? Not so much." He coughed. "We have to toughen up, Max. And we don't have a lot of time. Those babies will be arriving any day now, so I figured if I took some vitamin pills now and again by the time they drop us off at the pound I'll be all butch like Brutus or Clarice." He frowned. "I guess I took too many at once. Should have started with one, then ten, then take it from there. Plus, I thought they'd boost my love life, like I told you. If we're going to be on our own from now on I want a girlfriend."

"Oh, Dooley," said Odelia, stroking the small cat's fur. "I would never take you to the pound. And where did you get this idea about the babies?"

"But you and Chase…"

"Chase and I are simply boyfriend and girlfriend."

"But boyfriends and girlfriends have babies. Everybody knows that."

"Damn Discovery Channel," Grandma grunted.

"I promise you there are no babies on the horizon just yet," said Odelia gently. "And even if there were, nothing will change for you and Max. Your home will always be with me."

Dooley gave her a look of such hopefulness it almost brought tears to my eyes. "Do you promise?"

"Yes, I promise," said Odelia. "Babies or no babies, you'll always be my baby, too."

"Aww," said Marge softly, and even Tex's eyes suddenly grew moist.

"You're an idiot, you know that?" I told Dooley.

He sighed contentedly. "Yeah, but I'm Odelia's idiot."

Just then, Vena walked back in. "And how is our patient?" She checked Dooley and nodded with satisfaction. "His vital signs are fine. He'll be up and about in no time. I would like to keep him here overnight, though. Just to make sure he makes a complete recovery."

"I'll stay, too," I said quickly. No way was I going to let my friend stay in a creepy place like this. Clinics, whether for humans or for animals, always give me the heebie-jeebies.

"That's fine, Vena," said Odelia. "I know he's in good hands with you." She patted my head. "And if you don't mind, we'll leave Max here, too. He and Dooley are inseparable."

"Yeah, they're not your typical cats," Vena commented. "Most cats are solitary creatures. Not given to fraternizing with their fellow cats. Max and Dooley are different."

Odelia smiled. "They sure are."

This was the point when Vena told the Pooles that visiting hours were over and that it was time to let the patient get some healing shut-eye. She didn't put it in those exact terms, though, but still managed to shoo everyone out, which was a nice change of scene for us. Usually humans shoo cats out, and to see a human shoo other humans out was a lot of fun.

And then it was just me and Dooley.

"You didn't have to do this, Max," he said.

"Of course I did. You think I'm going to let you languish at this horror clinic alone?"

He gave me a startled look. "Horror clinic?"

"Sure. Aren't all clinics horror clinics?"

He conceded my point. "Do you think Vena does all kinds of weird experiments?"

"Wouldn't surprise me one bit."

A sudden sense of foreboding stole over me. I was at an animal clinic. A clinic for animals. Who knew what went on here when visiting hours were over? My flesh crept and flashes of a horror movie I'd once seen with Odelia returned to me. It was about a man who liked to experiment on the dead. *Re-Animator*, the movie was called, and scenes from the movie still creeped me out to this day. Particularly one disturbing scene where the doctor in charge of the proceedings reanimates a dead cat by injecting it with reanimator reagent.

Just then, Vena entered the room, and carefully closed the door behind her until it clicked into its lock. She was holding a huge syringe in her hand, and a strange and oddly disturbing expression on her face. Then she held up the syringe and pushed on the plunger, squirting some clear liquid from the needle. As she approached, she grinned ominously, syringe poised over her head, and then she grabbed for me. "Who's a good kitty-kitty?"

Both Dooley and I screamed, memories of *Re-Animator* returning in full force.

Barbara Crampton might be the scream queen, but we are definitely scream cats!

CHAPTER 30

O delia arrived at the police station just in time to see her uncle walk out with Tracy Sting on his arm. For a moment she thought she was seeing things. But then her uncle escorted Miss Sting to his pickup and gallantly opened the door for her and helped her in.

"Uncle? What's going on?"

Alec looked up, and so did Miss Sting. "Oh, hey, Odelia. May I introduce you to Tracy. Tracy, this is my niece Odelia."

"Hi, Odelia," said Tracy, getting out of the car again. "I've heard so much about you."

Odelia had trouble keeping her jaw reeled in. "But I thought—weren't you—didn't they—"

Alec smiled. "Oh, that was just a misunderstanding. All cleared up now I'm happy to say."

Odelia automatically shook Miss Sting—Tracy's—hand. "But... Burt Goldsmith..."

"Another little misunderstanding," Tracy said. "I explained all that to Alec."

"And once I explained it to Chase, he understood," said Uncle Alec.

"Understood what?"

"That I would never harm a hair on Burt's head," said Tracy. "After all those years on the road, staying in hotel rooms and traveling the country, Burt and I had become thick as thieves."

"Thick as thieves," Alec stressed.

"So you see, Miss Poole—"

"Odelia," Alec offered.

"Odelia, I would never hurt Burt. And I do hope you catch whoever is responsible."

"Oh, we'll catch the bastard," Alec assured her. "Just you wait and see."

Tracy placed a hand on his ruddy cheek. "I know you will, you handsome chief."

Odelia had heard her uncle be called many names but never this. And seeing him all loved up like this frankly astounded her. Furthermore, she wasn't as confident as he seemed to be that Tracy Sting wasn't the person they were looking for. She certainly was one tough baby, as far as she could determine. "Do you... have plans?" she asked, gesturing at the car.

Alec smiled at Tracy. "We're going out. Dinner and a movie. Isn't that right?"

"Something romantic," said Tracy. "The Rock has a new movie. Some *Die Hard* clone."

"I love *Die Hard*," said Alec. "One of my all-time favorite movies."

"Me too!" Tracy cried. "Another thing we have in common."

"Very romantic," Odelia agreed. She'd never seen her uncle look like a lovesick puppy before, and she decided that was just what he looked like right now. Well, maybe not a puppy. More a lovesick bulldog. "Just be careful, will you?" she said, not hiding her worry.

"Oh, we will," he said. "I'm always careful when I'm traveling with precious cargo." He gave her a wink, then practically raced to the other side of his pickup, a skip in his step, and hopped in, limber as a foal. "Ready, Tracy?"

"Ready when you are, Alec," Tracy said, and gracefully placed her shapely legs in the footwell of the truck before closing the door. She cranked down the window a few inches. "I'll take good care of your uncle, Odelia," she said with a purr to her voice. "Don't you worry." Then she gave her a wink and a smile and the odd couple were off at a healthy clip, Uncle Alec gunning the engine a few times for good measure. Like a young Bruce Willis.

Odelia stood staring after them, conscious of her head moving from side to side of its own accord. Moments later, she became aware of the presence of Chase next to her.

"We had to let her go," the cop announced somberly. "Alec insists she's innocent."

"He might be biased."

"You think?" He shook his head. "The woman has cast a spell on him."

"And he fell for it."

"Hook, line and sinker."

They stared after the chief's car as it disappeared around a corner with squealing tires and smoke pouring from the muffler. This wasn't good. "What if she blows him up?"

"She won't."

"She might."

"He's a grown man, Odelia. What do you want me to do? Tell him he can't go out with that girl? Tell him he's grounded and take away his phone and internet privileges?"

"Maybe we should tail them? Make sure she's not up to more funny business?"

"He'd spot us five minutes in. The man is a seasoned cop."

"I don't like it, Chase."

"I don't like it either, Odelia, but there's nothing we can do."

He was right. Just then, the cop's phone chimed. He put it to his ear, listened for a moment, then locked eyes with Odelia. He disconnected and put his phone away. A grin spread across his face. "I think we just caught a break, babe."

"What?"

"Crime scene people pulled a partial print from a bottle retrieved at the scene."

"And?"

"Curt Pigott."

CHAPTER 31

Turns out Vena wasn't The Re-Animator, nor was she The Exterminator or The Terminator or some other dastardly creature. Instead she was worried we wouldn't sleep well, what with being forced to spend the night in an unfamiliar environment, and had given us a mild sedative to make us relax and rest while Dooley recuperated from his ordeal.

And I might add that it worked. Soon after the terrible moment had passed—I hate shots, don't you?—I'd fallen into a deep and healing sleep and so had Dooley. When I woke up again it was because some altercation had occurred somewhere in the small clinic.

Vena's clinic is a modest affair. Two rooms and that's it. Dooley and I had gotten a nice comfy microfleece-lined perch to rest and recuperate on, accompanied by some of her other patients. I counted at least six: a puppy with mumps, a hamster with tendinitis of the elbow—those hamster wheels are a health hazard, I'm telling you—a parrot suffering a vocal issue, a parakeet with a beak sprain, a rabbit with toothache, and a pet mouse with pink-eye. Not that I could see the difference. As far as I know all mice have pink eyes. But I digress.

As I said, I was resting peacefully when all of a sudden I was awakened by the arrival of Vena with a fresh patient. It was another cat, this one of a more raggedy appearance. For a moment I thought it was Clarice, but when Vena finally left her modest ward, I saw it was a ginger cat, smaller and more diminutive than Clarice. When she caught me glancing over, she said, "Oh, hi. So nice to make your acquaintance. My name is Shadow. What is yours?"

I won't deny that I was stunned. For what felt like days we'd been searching high and low for this elusive Shadow, and now, through some strange twist of fate, here she was!

"Do you by any chance go by the moniker Most Fascinating Cat in the World?" I asked, holding my breath.

"I do, sir, yes. That's me. I'm the Most Fascinating Cat in the World. At least," she added, sagging a little in the soft and plush bed Vena had put her in, "I used to be. Before my human was blown to bits. Sad story, sir. Very sad story, indeed. Shall I tell it to you?"

"I think I know the story," I said. "Burt Goldsmith, right?"

"Best human a cat could ever hope to adopt. Bar none. Though I have to admit I also spent a lot of time with his grandson. Philippe Goldsmith. Have you made his acquaintance?"

"I have—though we were never formally introduced."

Next to me, another patient stirred. "Who is she, Max?" Dooley asked sleepily.

"Dooley, meet Shadow. Shadow, this is Dooley, my friend and housemate."

"And what is your name, friend?" asked Shadow.

"Max. Not the most original name, perhaps, but better than Princess at any rate."

"I used to know a Princess," said Shadow musingly.

"Most Compelling Cat in the World. Though not a very nice one, I'm afraid. If you ever do meet her, try to steer clear."

"We met," I said, "and I have the scratches and bites to prove it."

"I'm very sorry for your loss, Shadow," said Dooley. "We've been trying to solve your human's murder, but so far we haven't been able to."

"We got sidetracked," I admitted. "Some family drama that cropped up."

"Family drama will always crop up," Shadow agreed. "It did in my family, too. Like the time Philippe accused his grandfather of hogging all the attention and blocking his own rise to fame as the next Most Fascinating Man in the World. Or the time when Burt threatened to cut Philippe out of his will if he didn't stop annoying him with his constant nagging about taking retirement and allowing his grandson to take over his crown." She smiled. "Burt used to tease Philippe about being the Most Annoying Man in the World. Philippe didn't think it was funny. These things happen in every family," she assured us. "Best not to linger on it too much." She sighed. "Remember the golden nuggets and forget the darker moments is my advice. Before you know it your human is gone. Blown to bits by an exploding bottle of beer."

"You know about that?" I asked, surprised.

"I heard about it. You'd be surprised by the things one picks up when sleeping rough."

"You've been living on the street all this time?"

"I have. After what happened I was afraid to return to the hotel. When people start blowing up your human it's best to stay away. I don't enjoy the prospect of suffering the same fate, you see. I have this phobia about being blown up." She shuddered visibly.

"I think we all have a phobia about being blown up. Unpleasant experience."

"Isn't it?"

"Where were you when it happened?"

"Sleeping peacefully underneath the bed. Normally I sleep on top of the bed, but I like to change things up from time to time and that morning I'd opted to sleep underneath it. And a good thing I did. Suddenly the whole world seemed to come apart at the seams."

"How did you get out?"

"The connecting door had been blown off its hinges. I hid in there for a while, then out into the corridor the moment Philippe returned, and out through the fire escape."

"Philippe and his grandfather occupied connecting rooms?"

"Yes, they did. Philippe insisted on it. Said his grandfather was so old he needed to be nearby. In case something happened with his ticker. Not that Burt was fond of the idea. Said it cramped his style. Told his grandson that if he wanted to bring a couple of birds up to his room it was none of Philippe's damn business. Not that he ever did invite a couple of birds up to his room mind you," she added with the air of one harboring a secret regret.

"I think when he said birds he probably meant girls," I said.

This was news to Shadow. "Oh? Why? There's not even a remote resemblance."

"Humans," I said, and she nodded knowingly. So did every other animal in the room.

"Humans," they all echoed, and gave themselves up to silent reflection on the utter strangeness of the creatures that had adopted them as their pets.

"There's one thing I don't understand, though," said Shadow.

"Oh?"

"I saw that bottle of beer. I was there when it was brought in. And it smelled like beer. Being around Burt all those years I know what beer smells like, you see."

"I thought Burt didn't like beer? At least that's what my human said."

"He didn't. But you can't be the most famous beer salesman in the world and not sample your fair share of the brew over the course of all those years. And the beer that was brought in that day was beer. I remember peeping my head out from under the bed and taking a sniff, then retreating again. Moments later the door opened again and a powerful whiff of something else pervaded the room. It smelled like..." She wrinkled up her nose in distaste. "Burned sugar."

"Burned sugar?"

"I remember thinking, why would Burt burn sugar?"

"That must have been the nitroglycerin. You said someone else came in?"

"Yes. Unfortunately I didn't take a peek that time. And then Burt came walking in from the bathroom, mumbled something and that's when my whole world collapsed."

"And to think we thought we had it bad," said Dooley commiseratingly.

"Why don't you go back to Philippe?" I suggested. "He seems like a nice person, and I'm sure he's been looking for you everywhere. I know Odelia would if we went missing."

"Oh, Philippe is nice enough," Shadow admitted. "But he's not Burt. I liked Burt. Burt was fun. He always made me laugh by tickling my tummy and making funny faces." She smiled at the memory. "Philippe is different. He's a little grumpy. He doesn't make me laugh. I think it's because of all those headaches."

"Headaches?"

171

"He suffers from terrible migraines. Says it comes from his job as a teacher."

"He's a teacher?"

"A chemistry teacher. He loves his job but all those fumes he's inhaled over the years must have affected him adversely."

Shadow's words gave me pause. They seemed to stir a memory, but I couldn't quite catch it. Someone in the recent past had told me something about headaches. But who? And what? I shrugged it off. If it was important, it would come to me. For now I was content shooting the breeze with Shadow, who was possibly the most fascinating cat I'd ever met.

CHAPTER 32

The movie had gone down big with both Alec and his date. The Rock was a cop invited by accident to join the maiden flight of a billionaire's space ship because his ex-wife—The Rock's, not the billionaire's—now worked for him—the billionaire, not The Rock. But then a group of terrorists had interrupted the fun and killed the billionaire and taken his guests and the ex-wife hostage so The Rock had to fight his way through at least a dozen terrorists with a funny accent—the terrorists, not The Rock—before a sleazy reporter had exposed his wife—The Rock's, not the reporter's—to the terrorists and things had sort of deteriorated from there. Explosions, fist fights, gunfire, a lot of dead terrorists and of course the happy reunion. Alec was feeling on top of the world, and Tracy Sting evidently was, too, judging from the way she'd returned his heated kisses while the credits finally rolled.

"Wanna go back to my room for a nightcap?" she croakily asked when they walked out of the cineplex, fingers entangled.

"I sure do," he said just as croakily, though his croak was from emotion, not genes.

And they'd just stepped into her room and he'd pressed her up against the door, clothes magically dropping to the floor as if repelled by their heaving and grinding bodies when a knock on the door elicited annoyed groans from the both of them.

"Room service," a youthful voice announced.

Tracy yanked open the door. "What?!" she growled.

The pimply youth stared at her, and stammered, "N-n-nuts."

"Nuts?"

He thrust out a small glass dish of nuts. "N-n-nuts."

Tracy took it. "I didn't order no nuts."

"To go with the b-b-beer," the youth managed, before quickly retreating into the safety of the corridor.

Tracy slammed the door shut and stared at the nuts. "Weird. Did you order these?"

"Nope. Probably the same person who ordered those bottles of beer did," said Alec, gesturing at the amber bottles placed on a side table. They'd been there a little while, as they'd created a puddle on the table, condensation still producing droplets on the glass.

They both stepped up to the bottles and Tracy picked up the note that lay next to them. "Enjoy some real beer for a change," she read. "Taste the world's best brand. Signed Curt Pigott." Her brow furrowed. "Horrible little man," she grunted. "Can't stop taunting me." She picked up the bottles by the neck and prepared to dump them into a nearby trashcan.

"Hold on a minute," said Alec. "Let me take a whiff of those."

She handed him the bottles and he sniffed. "Doesn't smell like beer," he said finally.

Tracy, too, took a sniff. "More like... burned sugar," she said.

Their eyes met and Tracy carefully replaced the bottles on the table, then they were both backing away slowly towards the door.

Curt Pigott had just sent them two bottles of nitro-glycerin!

🐾

*C*hase pounded Pigott's door. "Police! Open up!"

Moments later, the World's Most Compelling Man appeared, his hair sticking up, his sleep mask askance on his brow, and one ear plug still sticking out of his ear, the other in his hand. He was looking slightly disheveled, trying to hold his robe gathered around his frame. "What's going on? Has there been another attack? I must have slept through it."

"There's been a breakthrough in the case," Chase announced.

"Oh, that's great! Have you caught the guy?"

"We have now," Chase said gruffly, and placed a hand on the man's shoulder. "Curt Pigott, you're under arrest for the murder of Burt Goldsmith." And as Chase read the startled actor his rights, Odelia looked sideways and then looked again, surprised when she saw her uncle, in a state of undress, accompanied by Tracy, also half-dressed, stalking towards her.

"Now, Uncle," she admonished him, "you can't keep doing this. The mayor won't like it when his principle crime fighter keeps showing up all over the place without his clothes."

"This man tried to murder us," Alec announced, pointing an accusing finger at Curt Pigott. "You sent two bottles of

175

exploding beer to Miss Sting's room just now. Don't try to deny it, you little shit!"

"They weren't bottles of beer," said Tracy, covering her modesty with her arms. "They were bottles of nitroglycerin."

Curt looked absolutely befuddled. "I didn't—I never—I wouldn't!"

"And yet you did!" Alec bellowed. "You're under arrest for the attempted murder of a police chief and his—his—his..." He glanced at Tracy, who crooked an amused brow. "His girl-friend!" he finished finally, and Tracy cast down her eyes, a smile playing about her lips.

"I never sent you any bottles!" Curt protested. "I'm inno-cent—innocent, I tell you!"

"Tell it to the judge," said Chase, who proceeded to cuff the compelling man.

"Good riddance," a voice spoke behind them. When Odelia turned she saw that they'd attracted quite the audi-ence: Bobbie Hawe, Jasper Hanson, Nestor Greco and Dale Parson all stood watching as their colleague and competitor was led away by Chase and Alec. "I've always known there was something fishy about him," said Nestor.

"Not me," said Dale. "I thought he was a kind man. Kind to animals and children."

"But not to interesting men," said Bobbie. "He likes to blow us up for some reason."

"Jealousy," opined Jasper. "Plain and simple jealousy. Couldn't stomach our success."

"Anyone up for a drink at the bar?" asked Nestor. "I'm buying."

And as Odelia watched the world's most interesting men head to the staircase, a discussion broke out amongst them over who was buying whom what type of beer. She shook her head and followed Tracy Sting to her room, to check on those beer bottles.

"Good thing your uncle has such a great sense of smell," Tracy was saying. "Otherwise we'd be dead right now. Blown to bits just like Burt."

"We better not touch anything," she said as she followed Tracy inside. She saw her uncle's shirt and pants on the floor and smiled to herself. The bottles looked exactly as Curt had intended them to look: like actual bottles of Tres Siglas. She crouched down to take a closer look, careful not to come near the dangerous objects.

"What I don't understand is why Curt would target me," said Tracy, pulling on a blouse and buttoning it up. "What could he possibly gain by murdering me and Alec?"

Odelia shrugged. "Looks like he was working his way through the competition one by one. His next targets were probably those other most interesting men."

"But why me? I'm not the competition."

"Yeah, I don't get that, either. Then again, who knows what's in the mind of a killer." She rose to her feet, and stepped away from the side table. "I'm sure Chase and Alec will make him talk. By this time tomorrow this whole ordeal will finally be over."

Police people were now entering the room, anxious to 'seal the scene' as they called it. Tracy nodded, then glanced at Odelia. "Any chance I can stay with you tonight? The hotel is booked solid, and Alec will probably be up all night questioning Curt Pigott."

"Sure. If you don't mind sleeping on the couch. I have a guest bedroom but my grandmother is staying with me at the moment." She grimaced. "Don't ask me why."

"I won't," said Tracy with a smile. "Alec told me some of it."

"He did, huh?"

"Yeah, for some odd reason he and I hit it off."

They walked out of the room as more police walked in. "He's a great guy," said Odelia.

"He is, isn't he? He's funny and sweet and... very, very passionate."

Odelia laughed. "He'll be happy to hear it. I don't think I've ever seen him this interested in a woman since Aunt Ginny died."

And then they were walking out of the hotel, and Odelia thought that this Tracy Sting wasn't as bad as all that. She definitely wasn't the murderous psychopath she'd initially taken her for. And then she found herself talking about her uncle, Tracy laughing at some of the stories, and before she knew it they were home and she was letting this perfect stranger into her house. And guess what? She didn't feel like a stranger to her. Not anymore.

CHAPTER 33

I shot up and cried, "Eureka!"

I know. It normally never happens to me, either.

But once I was up, I was wide awake, and so were Dooley and Shadow and all the other animals in Vena's nursery.

"I've got it!" I added for good measure. "It's you," I said, pointing at Shadow.

"Me? What did I do?"

"I don't mean you—I mean your human."

"My human? Burt?"

"Burt is dead, Max," said Dooley, as gently as possible. "You were having a nightmare."

"Not a nightmare," I said enthusiastically. "A brainwave!"

"Sounds dangerous," Shadow intimated. "Does it hurt?"

"I know who killed Burt!"

"It's the strain, Max," said Dooley. "You must have over-taxed yourself."

"No, I mean it. It's something you said."

"Me?" asked Dooley.

"Not you—Shadow."

"My shadow?"

"My name is Shadow," said Shadow.

"I know," said Dooley. "You told me—oh," he added. "You meant Shadow not shadow."

"Guys, will you quit yapping," said the pink-eyed mouse. "I need my beauty sleep."

"Yeah, all this crap is disturbing my biorhythm," chimed in the parrot hoarsely.

"It's cats," opined the hamster. "Always cats. They can't stop prattling. Prattle, prattle, prattle. That's why people hate cats but they all love a hamster. Hamsters are easy. We run on our little hamster wheel, snack from our little hamster nuggets and keep our traps shut."

"Will you shut up already," I told the Dr. Doolittle crowd. "I just solved a murder."

"Typical," mumbled the puppy. "Always bragging. That's cats for you."

"No, I really did. It was the boy that did it."

"What boy?" asked the rabbit, paw pressed to his painful cheek. "I'm not following."

"You don't have to follow. It's the kid that did it."

"The kid? Who's the kid?" asked the parrot.

"I don't care. I just want to sleep," said the mouse.

"Let's blow this joint, fellas," I said, suddenly feeling super-energized. I imagine that's why Sherlock Holmes often came across as suffering from ADHD. Solving a murder gives you this big jolt of energy to the brain. I jumped from my nice fleece-lined perch with some reluctance. Then again, I owed it to my human to give her the good news at once.

"Do we have to, Max?" asked Dooley plaintively. "It's so nice and warm in here."

"Yeah, I kinda like it here, too," said Shadow. "It's way better than life on the street."

"Don't you want to see the guy who killed your human arrested?" I asked.

Shadow thought about that for a moment. "Is this a trick question?" When I gave her a stern look, she finally relented. "Oh, fine. I'll play your little game. Where are we going?"

"Home," I told her.

"To the hotel?"

"No, a real home."

Dooley heaved himself up from his warm and comfy bed with a groan, then followed my lead. "You better be right about this, Max," he said. "I could get used to a place like this."

"What's happening?" asked the mouse, apparently waking up from a micro-nap.

"The cats are leaving," the parrot announced.

"Good riddance," said the mouse, and promptly dozed off again.

*H*alf an hour later we arrived at the house. Lucky for us Vena lives just around the corner. Cats aren't made to travel for miles and miles. Especially on an empty stomach.

"Good thing Vena left her window open," said Shadow, panting. "Or else we'd be screwed."

"Or lucky," Dooley muttered. He still wasn't on board with this whole plan of mine. Even though Odelia had promised him that, babies or no babies, she wasn't kicking us out, he wasn't completely convinced. And Vena seemed like a good back-up plan just in case.

We waltzed in through the pet door and I traipsed straight up the stairs. Odelia was sound asleep, as I'd expected. And she was alone, which I hadn't expected. No Chase. Where's the police when you need them? I pawed her intently, and when she didn't stir, used some claw to attract her attention. She pushed me away. "Not now, Max. I'm sleeping."

"But I know who killed Burt Goldsmith," I said, unable to contain my excitement.

"I do, too," she said, turning over to the other side. "It was Curt. Curt killed Burt."

That sounded more like a nursery rhyme to me, but then she was still half asleep.

"It wasn't Curt—whoever he is—it was Philippe! Remember how you told me Chase said nitroglycerin gives you terrible headaches? Well, guess who has terrible, debilitating headaches? Philippe! And guess who's a chemistry teacher? Also Philippe! And guess whose room was next to Burt's, with a connecting door. You guessed right! Philippe again! Shadow—oh, you haven't met Shadow, have you. She's Burt's cat. She was at Vena's. You'll like Shadow, Odelia. She's very nice. So Shadow told us she heard someone enter the room after room service dropped off that bottle of beer. I'm guessing it was Philippe, replacing the original bottle with one filled with nitroglycerin. He must have snatched that first bottle from the sap he'd chosen as his fall guy, leaving it in the room with the explosive bottle so this dude's fingerprints would be found at the scene. So you better arrest him now, Odelia!"

My long harangue was met with a soft snore. She'd fallen asleep in the middle of my exposé! Dang. I'll bet a thing like that never happened to Hercule Poirot when he delivered his closing statement, neatly wrapping up another case. Or Sherlock Holmes, for that matter.

I jumped down from the bed, and then trotted down the stairs.

I found Dooley and Shadow staring at a lumpy form on the couch.

"You guys, Odelia is out like a light. We'll have to wait until tomorrow."

"Max? There's a strange woman on our couch," said Dooley.

I checked the lumpy form and discovered that Dooley was right. There was a strange woman on our couch.

"It's Tracy," said Shadow. "Tracy Sting. She was my human's handler."

"Handler? You mean like a dog handler?" asked Dooley.

"Something like that. When Tracy said jump Burt asked 'how high?' Or at least that's the joke he liked to make. He was very fond of her. She's good people, Tracy is."

"But what is she doing in our house?" I asked.

"I guess we'll find out tomorrow," said Dooley with a yawn. "Let's sleep. I'm tired."

Just then, Brutus and Harriet walked in through the pet door. "Who's that?" Brutus asked, gesturing in the general direction of the couch.

"Burt Goldsmith's handler," I said.

"No, I mean the cat, not the dame."

"My name is Shadow," said Shadow courteously. "I was Burt's cat. Which means now I'm nobody's cat."

"Oh," said Harriet. "That's so sad." She turned to us. "Where have you guys been?"

"Long story. Dooley ate some of Brutus's pills and passed out."

"Brutus's pills?" asked Harriet. "What pills?"

"Nothing, nothing," Brutus hastened to say. "Listen, they finally caught this Burt guy's killer. Turns out some compelling dude killed him. And listen, *listen*," he said when I made to interrupt him, "someone tried to kill Uncle Alec by sending him an exploding bottle. Him and some babe he's seeing." He snapped his claws, or at least tried to. "Um, name escapes me."

"Tracy Sting," said Harriet. "That's her over there, sleeping on that couch."

"Right," said Brutus.

I thought about this. "Now why would Philippe try to kill Uncle Alec?"

"Philippe? Who's Philippe?" asked Brutus.

I was starting to feel a little tired. It's exhausting to be the most intelligent cat in the room. "Philippe is Burt's grandson. He killed his grandfather and now he's trying to kill Uncle Alec and..." My eyes narrowed. "You said Tracy Sting and Uncle Alec are an item?"

"An item?"

"A thing. A couple. Like Rose and Jack from *Titanic*," I said impatiently.

"I like Rose from *Titanic*," Dooley murmured wistfully.

"I don't know about that," said Brutus. "All I know is they were caught with their pants down steaming up the windows of Uncle Alec's car—we saw them, remember?"

I gave Tracy Sting's inert form a closer inspection. Brutus was right. This was the redheaded woman Uncle Alec was making out with in his squad car. And then I got it. "Philippe is taking out the competition."

They all stared at me. "Huh?" said Brutus.

"Don't you see? First Burt, now Alec, all the while making sure everyone thinks the Most Compelling Man in the World is responsible?"

"Curt Pigott," said Shadow helpfully. "He's the Most Compelling Man in the World."

So it wasn't a nursery rhyme. The police had actually arrested Curt Pigott for a crime he didn't commit.

"Why Alec?" asked Harriet. "That makes no sense to me whatsoever."

"It doesn't. It only makes sense to a mind as warped as Philippe's. He must have seen Uncle Alec and Tracy Sting and figured she was grooming him as the next Fascinating Man."

They all burst out laughing. All except Shadow. "Uncle Alec! Most Fascinating Man!" said Harriet. "You're joking!"

"It may sound like a joke to us, but it's not a joke to Philippe. Alec represents his competition, and he won't stop until he's dead. You guys," I said urgently. "We have to stop him!"

"Stop who from doing what?" asked Dooley, still experiencing the effects of Vena's treatment.

"Stop whom," Shadow corrected helpfully.

"Huh?"

"Not huh. Whom."

"Philippe," I said, my head starting to swim a little. "Stop Philippe."

"You all heard Max," said Shadow cheerfully. "Let's stop Philippe."

"Stop what?" asked Dooley.

"And why?" added Harriet.

"And who?" said Brutus.

"Whom," said Shadow. "Whommmmmm."

Ugh. I'll bet Hercule Poirot or Sherlock Holmes never had to deal with this crap.

CHAPTER 34

*O*delia was dreaming of her grandmother joining her and Chase in the middle of the night and getting in bed between them, effectively erecting a physical barrier between the couple, peevishly telling them they needed to behave and stop all this annoying cuddling.

She awoke with a start and for a moment felt disoriented, the world a strange place.

She patted the space next to her. No Chase. She checked the foot of the bed. No cats.

Odd. Where was everyone? Then the events of the past few hours came back to her. Dooley in hospital. The attempt on her uncle's life. The arrest of the Most Compelling Man. Max telling her something—whispering in her ear.

Had that been a dream? She could have sworn it was. Max was at Vena's. With Dooley. Spending the night.

So how come she vividly remembered him telling her that they'd arrested the wrong man? That it was in fact Philippe Goldsmith who was the real culprit? The one who killed his grandfather *and* tried to kill Alec and put the blame on Curt Pigott?

The more she thought about it, the more sense it made. She wasn't convinced, though. She needed more proof than the whispered words of a cat in the middle of the night. She was certain now she'd imagined Max. Dreamed him. Which meant that this was her subconscious at work—whispering in her sleep—warning her—wanting her to act now.

If Pigott was innocent, then whoever had tried to bomb Alec and Tracy was still out there—and could strike again at any moment. Which told her time was of the essence.

She rubbed her eyes, and checked her phone. Three o'clock. Probably too late to call her uncle and ask him about Pigott's interrogation. But not too late to call Chase. So she did.

His sleepy voice told her he wasn't at the police station interviewing Pigott.

"Is Granny bothering you again?" he asked. "Do you need saving?"

"Granny is probably sound asleep. I do need saving, though. From a hunch."

"A hunch."

"How did things go with Pigott?"

"Denies everything. Lawyered up."

"Struck out, huh?"

"We'll get him to confess. Lean on him a little harder tomorrow."

She bit her lip. "I'm starting to think you can lean on him all you want, he'll never break. Because he's not the guy we want."

"I know, babe. I'm the guy you want," he said, a smile in his voice.

"And I'm thinking we need to look a little closer at Philippe."

"Your granny's grandson? The Most Perfect Boy in the World? What makes you think so?"

"A hunch."

"Uh-oh. I know your hunches, Poole. They're freakishly accurate."

"Which is why I need you to do me a favor."

"Of course. I'll come over and brave Granny."

She smiled. "Maybe later. First I want you to check something for me."

"Now?"

"Now."

CHAPTER 35

"*And* that's why I think time is of the essence," I concluded my long speech.

The members of cat choir all stared at me, and so did the members of the Most Interesting Cats in the World troupe. As usual, they'd been hanging out at the park, limbering up those vocal chords, and practicing their dance moves. So when we joined them, the last thing they expected was to be treated to the kind of explanation usually reserved for the final scenes of a Hallmark Movies & Mysteries Channel presentation.

"You can't possibly expect us to believe you," said Princess, the first one to speak.

"I do, actually," I said.

"Max is right," said Shadow. "Philippe killed my human, and now he is after his next scalp."

"You're biased," said Princess. "I'm not listening to you."

"Of course she's biased," I said. "Her human was blown up. And now your human is in prison facing a life sentence for a murder he didn't commit. How can you sit there and pretend to be fine with that? If Curt Pigott goes to prison

189

your cushy life is over, Princess. You'll spend the rest of your days at the pound. Is that a chance you're willing to take?"

Princess gulped at this. "The pound?" she asked, her voice suddenly squeaky.

"Where all cats go to die," Dooley intoned gloomily.

"I don't want to go to the pound," Princess squealed, now only audible to dogs.

"You're not going to the pound," said the Most Iconic Cat in the World.

"There must be someone to take care of you when your human goes to jail," said Fat Amy, the Sexiest Cat Alive. "Someone—anyone?" she added when Princess gave her a look of panic.

"There's Leo, Curt's nephew, but he's a terror. Hates cats. Hates me!"

"Don't worry, Princess," said Beca, the Most Attractive Cat in the World. "I'm sure you can come and live with me. Bobbie will take you in."

"No, he won't!" cried Princess. "Bobbie hates Curt's guts. They *all* hate Curt's guts!"

"That's true," said Chloe, the Most Intriguing Cat in the World. "My human hates Curt. I heard him tell his mother that Curt going to prison is karma in action. And how he hopes to take over Curt's position as Most Compelling Man in the World. He wants to snag Curt's crown and become the Most Compelling Intriguing Man in the World. A real first."

"And don't think Philippe will stop here," I told them. "When he's done with Chief Alec he'll come after your humans next. He won't stop until they're all dead or in jail. And then he'll be the Most Fascinating, Compelling, Intriguing, Iconic, Attractive and Sexy Man in the World and all of you will be at the pound, wondering why you didn't try to stop him."

It was the kind of speech designed to rally the troops and

stir them into action, and I could sense that I'd hit the right note this time. Cat choir, meanwhile, was still looking at me like a bunch of lookie-loos, unlikely to be of any help to us or our mission whatsoever.

"And you," I said therefore, pointing at Shanille and company, "how many times has Chief Alec saved your hides? How many times has he called the fire department when you were stuck in a tree? How many times did he reprimand your human when they weren't treating you right? He's a good man, and now he needs *us* to save *him* for a change. So how about it? Are you with me?"

I would like to say that they reared up as one cat and yelled Yes! but unfortunately they did not. As I said before, cats are notoriously self-absorbed, and I'm afraid cat choir is no exception.

"What's in it for us?!" a raggedy tabby cried from the balcony—or, rather, a tree.

"Yeah, why would we stick our necks out for some stupid human?" shouted another.

"Free kibble for all!" suddenly piped up Brutus. "That's right," he added when all eyes turned to him. "If you help us out tonight there's free kibble for all as your reward."

"Who's gonna pay for that? You?"

"Uncle Alec will be so happy with what we did for him that he'll be happy to put on a feast to end all feasts," said Brutus. "I know the guy and that's just what he'd do."

"What kind of kibble?" asked a suspicious twenty-something old-timer.

"Yeah, not the generic kind. I get enough of that at home," said another.

"We want prime brand kibble or we ain't moving a paw!" cried a third.

"These cats are driving a tough bargain," said Brutus, blowing out a breath.

Finally I held up my paws. "Prime brand kibble for all!"

"Lifetime supply?" asked a cheeky little red cat.

"Don't push it, Brandon," Brutus growled.

"You cats should be ashamed of yourselves!" suddenly a voice rang out through the park. When we looked up we saw that Clarice had joined us. Perched high on a tree branch, she was looking down on cat choir, her fiery eyes shooting flame, her expression murderous.

"Clarice," said Shanille feebly. "What an honor."

Clarice is something of a legend in Hampton Cove's cat community. Feared and admired. Her appearance now was akin to the return of Luke Skywalker. If Luke Skywalker were a battle-scarred old warrior, living in self-chosen exile on the edge of our world. Oh, wait, he is.

"You weak, spineless, gutless bunch of sissy cats!" Clarice now thundered from her perch. "You shapeless blobs of self-indulgence! How dare you demand prime kibble in exchange for saving the life of the man who keeps this town running? The man who keeps the riffraff out? The man whose selfless-ness and sense of service is the stuff of legend? Whose commitment to Hampton Cove is the backbone of this community? Its very heart? You should be honored to serve the man who serves you. Not demand your pound of flesh!"

"More like a pound of kibble," piped up one cat, then ducked down his head shamefacedly when Clarice hissed in his direction.

"You're right, Clarice," finally said Shanille. "My human would say the same thing. Shame on you, Father Reilly would say. Shame on you for refusing to help a man in this, his hour of need. We need to come together as a community now and save one of our own."

It wasn't as effective as Clarice's speech, but heads were bowed, tails were tucked between legs, and finally it was agreed we should do what it took to save Uncle Alec from certain doom.

At least if I was right and he was, indeed, in mortal danger.

Admittedly I wasn't a hundred percent sure about that.

I was almost sure, though. Let's say ninety percent.

Maybe eighty. Possibly seventy…

Definitely fifty, though.

CHAPTER 36

*P*hilippe Goldsmith pulled up his collar. In spite of the late hour he wasn't absolutely convinced the streets were deserted. They should have been, but you never know with these sleepy little towns. Some old-timer might very well be up and about before dawn to walk his ratty old canine. Or some crusty old dame might be sitting at her window, cat in her lap, spying on the neighbors. Or a bird watcher, training his binoculars on a rare spotted owl.

And so it was that he furtively checked left and right as he walked on, his head retreating and emerging from his collar like a particularly timid turtle's. It didn't help that he had night vision trouble. During the daytime he saw just fine, but as soon as the sun went down the world turned a little blurry around the edges. He nervously pushed his glasses up his nose and squinted into the darkness that surrounded him.

There. Was that a cat meowing? When he stopped and turned, he thought he saw a furry form scurrying behind a tree, ducking out of sight. Weird. He'd never seen so many cats since his arrival in town. It was almost as if this freaky little place sported more cats than humans. They should have called it Cat Cove instead of Hampton Cove.

The weight of the cooler he was carrying hampered him in his progress. Not that it was particularly heavy, but the knowledge that at the slightest provocation its contents could blow him to kingdom come did much to make perspiration stand out across his hairline and drops of sweat to trickle down his spine.

But it had to be done. His life's work depended on it. He might not be his family's pride and joy, like Burt had been, but he was slowly getting there. If only the old man hadn't been so damn selfish. Wanting to keep going until he dropped—with never a thought to anyone but himself. But Philippe had taught the old coot a lesson he'd never forget. And now he needed to finish the job and show the world what a really fascinating man was capable of.

He giggled nervously, then jumped when another cat scooted out in front of him, almost tripping him up. He kicked at it, but the horrible furry creature was too quick.

He hated cats. Hated them with all the fervor of his being. Nasty little creatures. With their weird cat eyes that seemed to stare straight into your soul. And their sharp claws, ready to dig into your legs when they jumped onto your lap. Just like Shadow. At least she'd had the good sense to run off and drop dead someplace. Good riddance. And just when he was thinking about Shadow, suddenly he thought he saw her, sitting in a tree, staring intently.

He blinked, but when he looked again, she was gone.

He shook his head annoyedly. Damn those wretched eyes.

He slunk along the sidewalk and halted in front of a row house.

The lights were doused, as they should be. Alec Lip was sound asleep.

He wondered if Tracy was in there with the corpulent chief. She'd better be.

He snuck into the small patch of front yard, checked left and right again, put down the cooler and extracted the bottle from inside and placed it on the chief's doorstep, precariously balancing it against the door. The moment the chief opened his front door, the bottle would topple and kaboom! Bye-bye Most Fascinating Man in the World Wannabe!

He then retreated into the darkness across the street, but not before putting a note into the chief's mailbox. The mailbox would take a hit from the explosion, but the note would remain intact inside the metal box. When investigators found the note, signed by the Most Iconic Man in the World, they would have another suspect to turn their attention to.

Across the street from Chief Lip's house was a small patch of park, perfect for dog walkers, and he settled down behind a shrub and checked his watch. An hour was all it would take for the nitro inside the Seis Siglas bottle to defrost and become active again. One hour.

And as he prepared himself to wait, he became aware of those creepy night sounds all around him. As if nature was watching, and waiting, ready to pounce—just like he was.

And then he saw them. Cat's eyes, lighting up all around him. Dozens of them.

He shivered. Not from the cold, but from the sensation of being watched.

What did they want with him, these freaky cats? What were they waiting for?

Then he shook off the crazy notion. Sure, cats were watching him. Of course they were. Cats were just a bunch of dumb creatures. They were probably pissed he was trespassing on their terrain. Hogging their nocturnal hunting ground. Scaring away the mice.

"Shoo!" he whispered loudly. "Get away, you horrible creeps! Go on—get!"

They didn't move an inch, though. Just kept on staring at him, eyes unblinking and freaking him out in no small degree. Just what he needed. Bunch of cats getting on his nerves. He checked his watch again. An hour had passed. The time had come. And not a moment too soon. He got up stiffly and hurried over to the other side of the road.

Then he pressed his finger to the bell and pushed. Nothing. Not a sound.

He cursed silently. Dammit! Just his luck. The only house without a bell.

Good thing he had a back-up plan. He dashed across the street again, where the chief's pickup was parked and gave its tires a hearty kick. Nothing. He kicked the back panel and this time he hit the jackpot. The car's alarm started blaring so loudly it could probably be heard all the way to the other side of town.

He ducked back down behind his bushes, laying low, and watched with bated breath.

After a long moment, the lights went on inside the chief's house.

He watched on, giddy with anticipation. Any moment now. Any moment...

Just then, there was a loud meow, and suddenly a cat came hurtling out of the underbrush and raced across the street! It was a red cat, and a chubby one at that. But it still moved with marked agility and speed. It was going for the door—going for the bottle!

"No!" he cried, getting up from behind his hiding place. "You stupid cat!"

And then the cat launched itself at the bottle and jumped right on top of it!

Probably thought it was a frickin' mouse! Just his luck to encounter a kamikaze cat!

He ducked down, pressing his fingers in his ears. And then... nothing. No explosion.

He stuck his head out again, staring in horror and shock. The cat was kicking the beer bottle down the front yard, and the damn thing didn't explode! How was this possible?!

But then the front door opened and the chief stepped out. And then up and down the street doors opened and people appeared, annoyed by the blaring alarm.

Time to move.

Time to get the hell out of there.

And then he was speed-walking away, putting as much distance between himself and the chief's house as possible. They'd find the bottle and they'd find the nitro and the note and he wanted to be back at the hotel when they came to arrest the Most Iconic Man.

Just like the day when he'd blown up his grandfather. After he'd placed the bottle in the man's room, while Burt was in the shower, he'd quickly left the hotel via the fire escape, gone down around the back, and met this annoying reporter woman out in front, giving himself a nice solid alibi in the process.

And it was then that he discovered he was no longer alone.

That fat red cat was following him, meowing up a storm!

He walked faster, and the cat moved right along, now joined by a white cat, a small tabby and a big black cat that looked like it meant business. And as he broke into a trot, more cats joined the fray, and he saw that he was suddenly surrounded by the foul creatures! All around him they moved like a mass of fur! And then suddenly one of them jumped out of a tree and landed right on top of his head, claws extended, and dug in!

"Get off me, you horrible monster!" he cried, and tried to extricate himself from the clawed menace. "Get off!" He dragged the creature off and threw it away, but more cats used him as a climbing pole and suddenly they were everywhere! On his face, on his chest, digging their claws into his back. Dozens—hundreds! Thousands!

He stumbled and fell and his world turned into a nightmare of clawing and screeching monsters pressing him down, scratching his face, his hands, his neck!

"Get away from me, you beasts!" he roared, thrashing wildly. "Leave me alone!"

This was the stuff from a Stephen King novel! *Cujo: The Sequel*. This time with cats!

And then he heard the sound—the terrible sound.

Sirens. Police sirens.

He couldn't see a thing. The cats were all over him, blocking his view. Immobilizing him. Screeching up a storm. Going completely berserk.

The sirens stopped right next to him. Doors were slammed. Footsteps sounded.

And then a voice. A woman's voice.

"Well done, Max. You got him."

Suddenly, as if by command, the cats retreated.

When he had managed to adjust his glasses, he saw he was surrounded.

There was that annoying reporter—Odelia Poole. And Chase Kingsley, that equally annoying cop. And Chief Alec and Tracy. And more cops. Lots and lots more. He didn't even know a small town like this could have so many damn cops.

He gave them a feeble smile. "I was—I was out walking and I was attacked. Attacked by cats. Cats—cats gone crazy!" He emitted a laugh. It sounded shrill to his own ears.

Detective Kingsley didn't look convinced, and neither did the others.

"Philippe Goldsmith," said Chase in a rumbling undertone. "You're under arrest for the murder of your grandfather and the attempted murder of Alec Lip and Tracy Sting."

And as he was cuffed and led to a police car, an audience of cats was looking on, all along the street, sitting on tree branches and even lying on the roof of the squad car to get a better look. They were staring. Actually staring, unblinkingly. It was the freakiest thing.

And there was Shadow, giving him the evil eye as the cop tucked his head into the car.

And he could have sworn the little sucker's face was contorted into an actual smile.

The cat's lips moved, and before the car door was slammed shut, he thought he heard her say, "Gotcha!"

EPILOGUE

t was grill time at Tex and Marge's again. This time Chase had kindly offered the good doctor Tex his professional grilling expertise, probably hoping to dig his teeth into something more tasty than a charred sausage, scorched steak or blackened chicken skewer. Marge had made her fabled potato salad and Gran had actually baked no less than three apple pies.

Not that I cared. I'm not so big on potato salad or apple pie and I like my meat raw and juicy, not grilled to the texture of leather. And since Odelia knows how I like my food, she'd provided me and my fellow cats with some excellent nuggets of actual raw chicken.

Yes, I was the hero, fêted by all, and with good reason. Like some kind of action hero I'd actually thrown myself down on top of a live bomb. On closer inspection the bomb had been a beer bottle but I hadn't known that when I performed my act of heroism. I thought there was actual nitro in that bottle. And if Alec hadn't replaced the bottle of nitro with a bottle of Corona while Philippe Goldsmith wasn't looking, I'd have been dead by now.

But I wasn't, and anyway, cats do have nine lives, as everyone knows, so the explosion would have claimed only the one life, leaving me with eight more to regale my friends with the story of my exploits. And regale them I had. Wherever I went, cats wanted me to tell the story of how a cat had saved the day—and a couple of humans in the process.

"I'm telling you, Odelia," said Chase as he took the barbecue tongs from Tex and gave the doctor a gentle nudge in the direction of the bowl of sunset punch. Bourbon, vermouth, ginger beer, lemon and sugar. Even Tex couldn't mess that up. "Those cats of yours are something else. I still can't believe Max would throw himself on a bomb! Or maybe he thought it was a fat pigeon?"

"No, I think he actually thought it was a bomb," said Odelia, placing a bowl of apple and poppy seed coleslaw on the table. "And that he was actually saving Uncle Alec's life."

"And I for one am mighty grateful," said Uncle Alec, holding up a bottle of Corona in a toast to me. I would have held up my bottle but for one thing I don't drink beer and for another I was too busy sampling all the delicious foodstuffs Odelia had set out for us.

"I think it's amazing," said Chase. "Simply amazing. Did you give him some extra-crunchy kibble as a reward?"

"I gave him some extra-tasty chicken," said Odelia, throwing another juicy sliver in my direction. I deftly managed to snatch it from the air and gobble it down. Score!

"So how did you find out Philippe Goldsmith was the one you wanted?" asked Marge.

"Odelia called me in the middle of the night. Said she had a hunch Philippe might be the one," said Chase. "So I got on my computer and found he'd once burned down the school lab in some experiment gone wrong—the police report mentioned some type of home-made explosive he used that time. And only a few weeks before Burt's murder a garden shed blew up not far from the Goldsmith family estate. Luckily no one was hurt but police found traces of nitroglycerin at the scene, and a neighbor said a young man fitting Philippe's description had been seen hauling ingredients and equipment into the shed. He'd been experimenting for a while, trying to perfect the mixture he'd use on his grandfather."

"Why wasn't he arrested?"

"The Goldsmiths are a well-respected bunch, and the investigation was dropped."

"Someone paid the right person the right amount of money," said Tex.

"No amount of money will save him now," said Odelia. "This time he was caught in the act."

"Didn't you search his room after his grandfather was murdered?" asked Marge.

"We did. But since the explosion had happened in the next room it was only logical we found traces of nitro."

"Where did he keep his stash of explosives?" asked Tex.

"Hotel kitchen fridge," said Uncle Alec. "He'd told one of the servers his grandfather liked his beer cold, and had tipped the kid handsomely for the favor. He never had a clue."

"Clever."

"He was. Until someone saw right through him." He directed a look of admiration at Odelia.

"I think Max deserves all the credit," said Odelia. She couldn't tell Chase it was me who warned her about Philippe. It was her, though, who warned her uncle, and by the time Philippe arrived, police were at the scene, keeping a close eye on the amateur bomber.

"All's well that ends well," said Tex, and took a sip from the fruit punch and winced.

"So when can we get rid of these collars?" asked Harriet,

addressing the topic that interested her far more than humans trying to murder other humans.

"Right now," said Odelia, and proceeded to remove all of our collars!

"Burn them," said Brutus soberly, checking himself for fleas.

"Are they gone?" asked Dooley. "Are you sure they're gone?"

Odelia gave him a brief inspection. "All gone," she said. "Not a single one left."

"Oh, joy!" Brutus said, and did a little impromptu wiggle of his tush.

I took the butch cat aside. "How about your… issue?" I asked.

He gave me a wink. "What issue?"

I guess those pills Vena had dispensed had done the trick, for the moment he said it, Harriet sashayed over, and the two of them wasted no time stalking off into a laurel bush.

I hopped up onto the porch swing, turned around a few times, and took a seat next to Dooley. "I'm so glad those fleas are gone, Max," Dooley said, looking extremely relieved.

"Yeah, and I'm glad the Most Interesting Men in the World are gone, too, and they took their Most Interesting Cats along with them."

"Aren't you sad Shadow left?"

Shadow had been adopted by the Goldsmith family, and would live with Burt's second cousin twice removed, who was a genuine cat person. Tracy had promised Shadow a part in future beer commercials if she wanted. But the cat had decided to retire from the world of advertising. Acting in ads simply wouldn't be the same without Burt. Tracy, meanwhile, had also left, which made Uncle Alec a little sad. She'd promised to return, though, and maybe she would.

"It's fine," I said.

"But you liked Shadow," said Dooley. "She could have been your girlfriend."

"I doubt it."

"You'll always have #nitrogate, though."

I shrugged. I liked Shadow, I really did, but not in an amorous capacity. I guess the right cat for me is out there somewhere, and one day we'll meet. Maybe. I'm not holding out hope, though. Cats aren't like humans. We don't mate for life. We're more like George Clooney before he met Amal, or Leonardo DiCaprio before he meets the next hot young model. We like to play the field. Keep our options open, if you know what I mean. We're cats, for crying out loud. Not Ward or June Cleaver.

"What about you, Dooley?"

"What about me?"

"Still nervous about the baby thing?"

He blinked. "Why? Should I be nervous? Do you think Odelia lied to us? Max—is she going to kick us out?!" His voice was rising precipitously. "Tell me the truth! Is this the end?!"

Oh, boy. I should have kept my mouth shut. "No, it's not the end, Dooley. For one thing, as long as Gran stays at Odelia's, there won't be no babies."

Dooley glanced at Gran, who was stuffing her face with potato salad, as if she was the great white hope. Then he frowned. "I don't get it. What does Gran have to do with babies?"

"No young couple likes to be hassled by a live-in know-it-all granny cramping their style and sticking her nose in. No way Chase is moving in as long as Gran is in the house."

"I knew it," said Dooley. "I knew my human would save me. She's doing this for us, isn't she? She's trying to keep those babies from muscling us out of the house."

"No, she's not. She's pissed at Tex and Marge and trying

to get back at them for not supporting her claim to Gold-smith fame and fortune. She'll move back out at some point."

"When?!" he cried.

I shrugged. "When she feels Tex has suffered enough."

We both directed a curious look at Tex, who was humming a pleasant tune, looking pleased as the punch he was serving. "Tex doesn't look like he's suffering, Max," Dooley said.

"Tex has never been happier. He's finally managed to achieve the one thing he's always wanted: kick his mother-in-law out of the house. Tex is living the dream right now."

"Which means… Gran will live with Odelia forever! This is good!"

I transferred my gaze to Chase, who looked decidedly unhappy. Which just goes to show that one man's dream is another man's nightmare. Frankly I didn't care either way. Chase moving in or Chase moving out. Gran moving out or Gran moving in. Babies or no babies. I knew that Odelia would always have my back and so would the rest of the Pooles and the Lips. They'd saved me from an exploding beer bottle and I'd done the same for them. In other words, it was all good.

And as I watched my humans tuck in and be merry, I placed a paw around Dooley's shoulder. "Relax, buddy. Babies or no babies, we'll always be Odelia's pets. And who knows? If a pack of wild babies should happen to pop up one day all it would mean is more humans to buy tasty bits of kibble for us, right? And more humans to cuddle us and spoil us rotten."

He eyed me with surprise. "You really think so, Max?"

"I know so. You know what I heard? That babies *love* cats. Absolutely adore us."

He thought about this. Hard. I could tell from the whirring sound his brain made. Then something clicked and he nodded solemnly. "All right, Max. I'm ready to have a baby."

THE END

You're probably wondering about the identity of 'Patient Zero,' the cat who started the Great 2018 Flea Disaster. In Purrfectly Flealess, a 15.000 word short story, our fearsome foursome go in search of this First Fleabag. The answer to the mystery will shock them to their very whiskers... Read on for a three-chapter excerpt.

EXCERPT FROM PURRFECTLY FLEALESS

Chapter One

We were out in the backyard of Odelia's house, undergoing what at first glance to any observer would have appeared an extremely humiliating procedure: Odelia had put a large washtub on the lawn, had filled it with warm soapy water, and was meticulously dragging a comb through the water and through my fur in an effort to catch those last, hard-to-reach fleas that might still linger on my precious bod. Meanwhile Marge was doing the same with Harriet, and Grandma Muffin with Dooley. Brutus, the fourth cat in our small menagerie, was doing his business in the bushes, waiting for his turn.

"And? Did you find any?" I asked, getting a little antsy.

As a general rule I hate getting wet. Odelia had assured me this washing time business was for the greater good, though, so I had agreed to go with it. Just this once.

"So far so good," she said as she carefully inspected the comb.

"Why isn't Brutus getting waterboarded?" I asked. "It's not

fair. We're all getting waterboarded and he's getting away scot-free. I think Chase should waterboard his cat."

"It's not waterboarding," Odelia explained. "It's just a gentle grooming session."

"Whatever," I grumbled, as I watched Dooley patiently undergoing similar treatment.

"I like it," my friend said. "As long as it gets rid of these fleas I'm all for it."

"I agree," said Harriet, who now sported a dab of foam on the top of her head. "Anything to get rid of these hairy little monsters is all right by me."

"Hairy?" asked Dooley, his eyes widening. "Nobody said anything about hairy."

"Oh, yes," said Harriet. "Fleas are big, hairy monsters, Dooley. As hairy as they come."

Dooley gulped. "Get them off me, Grandma. Please get them off me!"

"Hold your horses," Grandma grunted as she squinted at the comb. She then held it up for her daughter's inspection. "Do you see anything on there, Marge? Those little suckers are so small I can't be sure."

Marge studiously ignored her mother, though, and continued combing Harriet as if Grandma hadn't spoken. Ever since the old woman had decided to leave Hampton Cove to go and live with her newly acquired grandson, Grandma Muffin was dead to Marge.

Undeterred, Grandma waved the comb in Marge's face. "Is that a flea or a piece of lint? I can't tell."

Marge finally took a closer look at the comb, a dark frown on her face. "Unless it's an imaginary flea, like your imaginary pregnancy, there's nothing there."

"Suit yourself," Grandma grumbled, and went back to dragging the comb through Dooley's gray mane. She was using ample amounts of soap, and Dooley was now starting to resemble a drowned rat, hunted look in his eyes and all. "I'll have you know that that was a great opportunity, Marge, and if you'd have been in my shoes you'd have gone for it, too."

Marge turned on her mother. "No, I wouldn't. I would never leave my family to go and live with a bunch of strangers just to get my hands on a little bit of money."

"It wasn't a little bit of money," said Gran. "it was a lot. A big ol' bundle of cash."

"Even so. You don't leave your family just because you happen to strike it rich."

"I would have brought you in on the deal eventually," said Gran.

Marge planted a fist on her hip. "And how would you have done that?"

Gran shrugged. "I would have hired you as my maid or something, and Tex as the chauffeur. That way you could have lived in a little room over the garage. Shared the wealth."

Marge pressed her lips together and made a strangled sound at the back of her throat. Living above the garage and working as her own mother's maid didn't seem to appeal to her all that much.

"Dad is a doctor, not a chauffeur, Gran," Odelia pointed out. "And Mom is a librarian, not a maid."

"Who cares? The Goldsmiths got money to burn. He wouldn't have had to do any chauffeuring. Just pretend to go through the motions. Maybe wash a limo from time to time. Wear one of them snazzy peaked caps. Just saying. This family missed a great opportunity."

"We didn't miss anything," said Marge. "All we missed was you going off and showing your true colors."

Brutus had returned from his business in the bushes, and was stalking across the lawn with the air of a cat whose bowel movements have just proved a source of great enjoyment. If he'd been a human male he'd have carried a newspaper under his arm, folded to the sports section. When he caught sight of the flea party in progress on the lawn, the smile of contentment faded and he started backtracking in the direction of the bushes again.

Marge's eagle eyes had spotted the big, black cat, though. "Oh, Brutus, there you are. Come over here a minute, will you? We need to check you for fleas."

"I ain't got no fleas," he said promptly. "No, ma'am. I'm officially flea-free."

Marge smiled indulgently. "Be that as it may, you still need checking out. Now come over here and I'll give you your checkup."

"Does that mean you're done with me?" asked Harriet with a note of disappointment in her voice. Harriet likes being pampered and groomed. The more pampering the better.

"Yup. All done," said Marge.

"Oh," said Harriet, and reluctantly relinquished her spot to her beau Brutus.

"You know?" said Dooley as he directed a fishy look at a floating flea. "I'm not so sure this is an entirely humane way to treat these animals, Max."

"What animals?" I asked as Odelia lifted my tail and checked my rear end.

"Well, we're all God's creatures, Max, so maybe all this poisoning and waterboarding and generally slaughtering these poor fleas isn't the way to go is what I mean to say."

We all stared at the cat. Even Grandma momentarily paused her combing efforts. "You're nuts," was her opinion. "I've got a nut for a cat."

Odelia, however, seemed prepared to give Dooley the

benefit of the doubt. "I thought you didn't like fleas, Dooley? You couldn't wait to get rid of them?"

"Oh, I do. Hate the little parasites, I mean. And I do want to get rid of them. But maybe we should go about this the humane way. Treat them with kindness. Humanely."

"Whatever," said Harriet with a flick of her tail as she licked those last few droplets of water from her shiny white fur. "As long as they're gone, it's fine by me." She then gave me a censorious look. "So have you found your Patient Zero yet, Max?"

I looked up, distracted by Odelia dragging her comb across my sensitive belly. "Huh?"

"Patient Zero," Harriet repeated impatiently. "I thought you and Dooley were trying to track down the cat who got us into this mess and deal with him or her properly?"

"Yeah," I said vaguely. "We're, um, working on it."

"Well, work faster," she said. "I don't want to go through this ordeal again."

"Are you really tracking down Patient Zero, Max?" asked Marge.

"Sure, sure," I said. Actually I'd totally forgotten about this elusive Patient Zero. Like Harriet said, as long as the fleas were gone, who cared about Patient Zero, let alone patients one or two or three or whatever? "We're looking into it, aren't we, Dooley?"

But Dooley was still thinking about the fate of those poor fleas. "I mean, if the Humane Society cares so much about horses and the way they're treated in all those Hollywood movies, shouldn't they look into fleas, too? We're all God's creatures, right?"

Brutus emitted a groan. "Fleas aren't creatures, Dooley. Fleas are a pest. And pests should be terminated. End of discussion."

"Fleas deserve our consideration, Brutus," said Dooley

with a pained look as he watched a flea float lifelessly in the tub. "Have you ever stopped to consider that this flea right here has a mother and a father who care about him or her? And brothers and sisters?"

"Lots and lots of brothers and sisters," said Odelia with a slight grin. "Millions of them. Probably billions or even trillions."

"We still owe it to them to treat them with kindness and respect," Dooley insisted.

Odelia held up her comb. "This is being kind, Dooley. This is being respectful."

"Kind and respectful," Gran scoffed. "They're not being kind when they suck your blood, are they? So why should we be kind to them?"

"Kill 'em all is what I say," said Brutus, with a decisive motion of his paw. "Carpet bomb the suckers to oblivion."

"Speaking of carpets, did you take the vacuum bags out to the trash?" asked Marge. "They're probably full of eggs, larvae and pupae. Best to get rid of them immediately."

And so the discussion went on for a while. Harriet wasn't to be deterred, though. She was directing a scathing glance in my direction. I rolled my eyes. She wasn't going to let this go, I could tell. She was going to hound me until I produced this mysterious Patient Zero.

"Fine," I said finally. "We'll find your Patient Zero and we'll find him today, all right?"

She smiled. "Thanks, Maxie. I knew you'd listen to reason. Brutus and I will join you. And together we'll search this town until we've tracked down the cat who's responsible for this terrible outbreak and make sure he or she is unflead ASAP."

"I don't think unflead is a word, honey," said Marge.

Harriet flapped her paws. "Deflead, then. Whatever. But mark my words, I won't rest until the last flea of Hampton

214

Cove has been terminated." When Dooley gasped, she quickly added, "in the most humane and kindest way possible, of course."

Chapter Two

The moment we were finally declared flea-free, the four of us set out to start hunting high and low for Patient Zero and 'take care of him,' in Harriet's words. She seemed pretty sure this Patient Zero was a male, as only males could be so dumb as to allow themselves to be infested with a bunch of lowly parasites.

"And it's not just that the female of the species is smarter than the male, we're more hygienic, too," she claimed now as we tracked along the sidewalks of Hampton Cove. "I for one would never allow even a single flea to lay its eggs on my precious fur if I could help it."

"None of us would allow that," I countered. "Do you think I like hosting a flea party?"

"You tomcats are simply too insensitive to even feel that you're being ravaged by a bunch of parasites," she said, tail high in the air as usual. "You could have thousands of fleas feasting on your bodies and you wouldn't even know. But put one flea on me and I'll know instantly that something is wrong. Admit it, Max, females are much more conscious of their bodies than males."

"Like the princess and the pea," said Dooley, much to my surprise. When we all looked at him, he shrugged. "She could feel the pea, which showed everyone she was a princess. The same way Harriet can feel the flea, which shows us she's..." He swallowed, and his cheeks would probably have flushed a bright scarlet if they hadn't been covered in fur.

"Aw, Dooley," said Harriet. "You think I'm a princess? That's so sweet of you."

Brutus gave Dooley a dirty look. Its meaning was clear: she's my princess, buddy, so paws off.

We passed along the streets of Hampton Cove, the sleepy little town in the Hamptons where life is lived at a more leisurely pace than in other small towns the world over. This morning was different, however, with the sound of vacuum cleaners working at full tilt audible wherever we pointed our antenna-like ears. Windows had been flung open, with duvets, comforters and mattresses hanging from ledges, soaking up the sun's rays, carpets being cleaned with a frantic energy that told us the flea infestation had left the good people of Hampton Cove scrambling. Some people were even fogging and fumigating their houses, judging from the clouds of acrid smoke wafting through windows and doors and chimneys.

Dooley shook his head. "Maybe we should call the Humane Society, Max. I think they'd have a field day fighting all this cruelty and this utterly senseless suffering."

"How long do you think a flea can survive inside a vacuum bag?" asked Harriet.

"Not long," said Brutus. "I imagine they die a slow and painful death of suffocation."

Dooley uttered a strangled cry. "Oh, those poor, poor creatures."

"They're a pest," Brutus grunted. "And pests should be eradicated. No mercy."

"Some people consider cats a pest," I said. "They feel we should be eradicated."

"Some people are pests," Brutus countered. "So maybe they should eradicate themselves."

"Oh, but they do," said Harriet. "People kill each other all the time. They enjoy it."

She was right. Only a couple of days ago a grandson had killed his grandfather, just so he could take over the old man's title as Most Fascinating Man in the World. No cat would ever kill another cat for the mere pleasure of being called Most Fascinating Cat in the World. Humans sometimes can be quite inhumane. Before I could ponder the topic more deeply, however, we'd arrived in the heart of town, and Brutus and Harriet took one side of the street while Dooley and I took the other. We were looking for clues revealing the identity of this Patient Zero, and what better way to go about this pursuit than to talk to other cats?

Cats, as you might imagine, are extremely chatty creatures. There's nothing a cat likes better than to gossip about his or her fellow cats. And since our human is in the business of providing fresh human gossip to other humans every day through her column in the Hampton Cove Gazette, that works out quite nicely. So we passed by the barber shop and talked to the barber's Maine Coon Buster, who sat licking his paws in front of the shop.

"First time I laid eyes on a flea I was a young whipper-snapper of six months," he said with a faraway look in his eyes as he temporarily halted his grooming. "My pa showed me. Said a cat's not a cat without a bunch of fleas burrowing into his skin." He sighed wistfully. "Ma kicked him out of the house that day and I haven't seen him since. I miss my old man sometimes. Said he'd fathered a thousand kittens in his time, and felt ready and primed to father a thousand more. Which is probably why Ma kicked him out in the first place."

"That's all fine and dandy," I said, trying to halt the stream of words. Buster likes to gab, and sometimes it's hard to get him to focus. "But we're trying to figure out when this flea infestation started, so try to cast your mind back to when you saw the first flea now—not when you were a young whipper... snipper."

He dabbed at his eyes with his paws. "He said he'd be back for me, Pa did. But I never saw him again. I sometimes wonder if he's out there somewhere, looking up at the same stars at night, thinking about me and those fun times we shared back in the day."

"If he fathered a thousand kittens and was ready to father a thousand more it's highly unlikely he remembers you, Buster," said Dooley, offering his two cents.

Buster stopped rubbing his eyes and gave Dooley a nasty look. "Who asked you?"

"It's simple logic," Dooley argued. "How can a cat be expected to remember one cat out of thousands? And I'll bet you were not very memorable at six months. None of us are."

"Dooley," I told him warningly.

"I stood out amongst the bunch," said Buster through gritted teeth. "Even as a kitten."

"I'm sure you did, Buster," I said pacifically. "Now about this Patient Zero…"

"Are you telling me that my pa never gave me a second thought? Cause let me tell you, you scruffy-faced piece of no-good mongrel, he did. Pa said he'd be back for me and the only reason he would break that promise is if he was detained someplace, unable to come."

"Probably fathering his ten-thousandth kitty," said Dooley. "Or taking a breather. Fathering so many kitties causes a lot of wear and tear. Your pa probably hung up his spurs."

"Why, you little…" Buster began, swinging his paw. "I should knock your whiskers off."

"Now, now," I said. "We're all friends here."

"Just buzz off," said Buster, giving us a distinctly unfriendly look.

And as we walked away, Dooley asked, "Is it something I said, Max?"

"No, Dooley," I said with a sigh. "But maybe from now on

you'll let me do the talking, all right? We are trying to find Patient Zero, not looking to start a fight."

"Okay, Max. I was just pointing out a flaw in Buster's logic, that's all."

"I know you were, Dooley. I know you were."

Chapter Three

Next up was Tigger, the plumber's cat, who, for some reason, sat people-watching on the stoop of Daym Fine Liquor, the local liquor store.

"Hey, Tigger," I said by way of greeting. "What's new?"

Tigger, a small hairless cat, held up his paw and I high-fived him. "Hiya, fellas," he said. "Just waiting on my human. My human likes this store. In fact it's his favorite store in all of Hampton Cove. He's in here all the time so I'm out here all the time."

"Why?" asked Dooley, who was in an inquisitive mood today. "You're not a dog. You're not supposed to sit out here and wait for your human."

"Oh, I know I'm not a dog," said Tigger. "But once Gwayn has some liquor in him he tends to forget he's got me to feed, so I like to trail him to remind him I'm still here."

It was an intensely sad story, though Tigger didn't seem to see it that way, judging from his chipper demeanor. Just one of those things cats take in their stride, I guess. When your human is a tippler, like Gwayn Partington obviously was, a cat learns to adjust.

"We're looking for Patient Zero," Dooley said, getting straight down to business.

"Maybe check the hospitals?" Tigger suggested. "That's where they keep those. I know on account of the fact that Gwayn has been in one. He has balance issues, you see, and tends to fall on his face from time to time. It's a terrible affliction. Every time it happens an ambulance comes and a couple of men in white take him down to the hospital."

"We're not looking for a particular patient," I clarified. "We're looking for the first cat in Hampton Cove who got infested with fleas. If we can track him or her down, we might be able to nip this thing in the bud, so to speak. Eradicate this infestation once and for all."

Tigger shook his head. "I'm sorry to disappoint you, fellas, but you can't eradicate a flea infestation. Fleas are everywhere! Fleas are all around, just like in the song."

"Song? What song?" I asked.

"Fleas are all around," he began to sing to the tune of *'Love is all around.'*

"They weren't before—not on this massive scale. Someone brought them here."

He stopped singing and gave me a pensive look. "Maybe ask Chief Alec? If anyone knows what's going on in Hampton Cove it's Chief Alec. Chief Alec knows. And he's nice to cats. I should know. The other day, when Gwayn spent the night at the police station, Chief Alec drove over to the house and gave me a saucer of milk and a piece of his ham sandwich. What a mensch!"

"Gwayn spent the night at the police station?" I asked.

"Sure. He was driving through town when he happened to drive through a red light—Gwayn suffers from color-blindness as well as this falling-on-his-face thing, you see—and so Chief Alec made him walk a line. Apparently that's what they do when people drive through red lights—make them walk a line. He must have aced the test because the Chief was so kind to offer Gwayn free lodgings at the police station for the night. Like I said, a real mensch."

Just then, Gwayn Partington came staggering out of the liquor store, a big brown paper bag in his arms, and stared down at us. "Well, I'll be damned," he muttered. "First there was one cat and now there's three? I must be off a damn lot worse than I thought!"

We watched as Tigger's human stumbled down the street, his hair sticking up, his bushy beard unkempt, and his blue coveralls a little too tattered to appeal to the average client of his plumbing business. Tigger sighed. "I love my human, I really do, but he doesn't make it easy." He turned and started in pursuit of the sauced plumber. "See ya, fellas. And if you see this Patient Zero of yours, tell him next time he should keep his fleas to himself."

"Wait, I thought you didn't believe in this Patient Zero theory?" I yelled after him.

"If you believe it, I believe it!" he yelled back, and gave us a cheerful wave.

"He's a real philosopher, this Tigger," said Dooley admiringly.

"With a human like that, you have to be," I said.

"Do you think Gwayn Partington is an alcoholic, Max?"

"Either he's an alcoholic or a method actor getting into character as an alcoholic."

We traipsed on, dodging pedestrians as we did, until we reached the Vickery General Store, where two cats sat shooting the breeze in front of the store. They were Kingman, generally accepted as the best-informed cat in Hampton Cove, and a ratty little cat called Kitty. She belonged to a local landscaper and was explaining something to Kingman while gesticulating wildly.

"And then he locked me up in the washer. The washer! Can you imagine?!"

I'd heard the story before so I wasn't all that interested. Still, being locked up in a washing machine is one of those universal horror stories that gives cats the creepy crawlies.

"Her human locked her up in the washer," said Kingman, jerking a paw to Kitty. "Can you believe it? What an idiot."

"At least you didn't get fleas," I said.

"Fleas don't kill you, tough guy," said Kitty. "The washer will. Unless you're me, of course." She shook her head. "No idea how I survived that one. I must be one tough kitty."

"Maybe your Odelia should write a story about that," Kingman suggested. "I mean, all she ever writes about is humans doing stuff to other humans, but when is she finally going to write about the things that really matter? Like getting stuck in a washer, huh? Or this flea infestation? That's the stuff I would like to see featured on the front page once in a while."

"He's right, you know," said Kitty. "I mean, take that big story that's been all over the news these last coupla days. About that Most Fascinating Dude that got killed by some other Most Fascinating Dude. Who cares, right? I don't. Dudes be killing dudes all over the place all the time. But how often do you get to talk to a cat that survived three washing cycles?"

"You survived three washing cycles?" I asked.

"It sure feels like it! But do I get asked for an exclusive interview? No, sir! No fair!"

"You should tell Odelia to give me a call," said Kingman, tapping my chest smartly. "I have an interesting story to tell about the flea epidemic. A story that would rock this town."

"Or she could call me," said Kitty. "A cat that survived four washing cycles!"

I stared at Kingman, hope surging in my bosom. "You know something about this flea thing?"

"Sure I do," said the voluminous piebald, and wiggled one of his chins for emphasis. "Mark my words. If what I have to say gets printed in the Hampton Cove Gazette the good people of this town would be shocked. Shocked, I tell you!"

"Not as shocked as I was after surviving five washing cycles!" cried Kitty.

"Do washing machines even go through five washing cycles?" I asked.

"Ten! A dozen! If not more!"

"Just the one," said Dooley. "I know because I love to watch the machine go round and round."

"All cats love to watch the machine go round and round," said Kingman.

"Well, my human's machine goes round and round at least two dozen cycles," said Kitty adamantly, "and I survived every single one of them. So there." And having said this, she stalked off, ready to pounce on the next cat and start telling her story all over again.

"Look, Kingman," I said. "We're on a mission, Dooley and I. A mission to find Patient Zero. So better tell us everything you know about this flea infestation and better tell us now."

Kingman nodded soberly. "It was a dark and stormy night…" he began.

END OF THIS EXCERPT

This short story is now available as part of Max's second short story collection. Enjoy!

ABOUT NIC

Nic has a background in political science and before being struck by the writing bug worked odd jobs around the world (including but not limited to massage therapist in Mexico, gardener in Italy, restaurant manager in India, and Berlitz teacher in Belgium).

When he's not writing he enjoys curling up with a good (comic) book, watching British crime dramas, French comedies or Nancy Meyers movies, sampling pastry (apple cake!), pasta and chocolate (preferably the dark variety), twisting himself into a pretzel doing morning yoga, going for a brisk walk, and spoiling his feline assistants Lily and Ricky.

He lives with his wife (and aforementioned cats) in a small village smack dab in the middle of absolutely nowhere and is probably writing his next 'Mysteries of Max' book right now.

www.nicsaint.com

Made in the USA
Coppell, TX
22 August 2024